Praise for th

"Solid tween ap

"... a pre-Steven King novel for tween readers."
– BellaOnline.com

"... a storyline that fantasy addicts will devour."
– *Montreal Review of Books*

"[An] appealing mix of realism, whimsy, and legend."
– *Booklist*

"... bubbles along at a magical pace ... creepy enough to cast a spell over anyone who reads it!"
– *Resource Links*

"DeMeulemeester has scored big ..." – *Vancouver Sun*

"Cat is an engaging heroine, and Grimoire has just the right amount of evil ..."
– *January Magazine*

"... an entertaining and worthwhile read." – *Kirkus Reviews*

"We simply want to devour more of this author's highly readable and intriguing prose that she has a knack for creating ... Next installment, please!"
– *CM: Canadian Review of Materials*

Visit the official "**Grim Hill**" series website:
www.grimhill.com

Grim Hill
Forest of Secrets

written by
Linda DeMeulemeester

Lobster Press ™

Grim Hill: Forest of Secrets

Published by Lobster Press™
1620 Sherbrooke Street West, Suites C & D
Montréal, Québec H3H 1C9
Tel. (514) 904-1100 • Fax (514) 904-1101 • www.lobsterpress.com

Publisher: Alison Fripp
Editor: Mahak Jain
Editorial Assistants: Stephanie Campbell & Simon Lewsen
Cover Illustration: John Shroades
Graphic Design & Production: Tammy Desnoyers
Production Assistant: Vo Ngoc Yen Vy

We acknowledge the financial support of the Government of Canada through the Canada Book Fund for our publishing activities.

Library and Archives Canada Cataloguing in Publication

DeMeulemeester, Linda, 1956-
Grim Hill : forest of secrets / written by Linda DeMeulemeester.

(Grim Hill ; #5)
ISBN 978-1-926909-87-5

I. Title. II. Title: Forest of secrets. III. Series: DeMeulemeester, Linda, 1956- . Grim Hill ; #5.

PS8607.E58G746 2011 jC813'.6 C2010-906441-0

Printed and bound in Canada.

BIO GAZ ENERGIE Text is printed on 100% recycled post-consumer fibre.

Remembering Dawn Marie Holtby (Ellis) and Ryan Edward Holtby
– Best friends forever

... That is why falling stars are visible for a split second,
They hope against hope that their light will be seen,
And that someone will catch them.
And put them close to their heart,
And again make their fire start.
So that again they can shine bright,
Bringing joy, love, and laughter to all those near their light.

– Ryan Edward Holtby

Acknowledgements

Much appreciation to everyone at Lobster Press for all their hard work on the Grim Hill series, with special thanks to Alison Fripp and Stephanie Hindley. Thank you to Mahak Jain and her assistants, Stephanie Campbell and Simon Lewsen, for their insightful editorial feedback! John Shroades, your covers are pure enchantment. Love to John, Alec, and Joey.

– Linda DeMeulemeester

Chapter 1

Uneasy Beginnings

THE TALL GRAY lockers of Shadowridge High loomed over me while my friends and I waited for Jasper to leave the library. I rubbed my clammy palms against my jeans. Call it déjà vu. I'd started a new school before and I knew from experience it wasn't fun.

I swallowed. *Courage, Cat,* I told myself. *After all, just the day before you were looking forward to this.*

"Wow, this school is a lot bigger than Darkmont," Amarjeet said. The edge in her voice made me think I wasn't the only one who had butterflies backflipping in her stomach.

This place was huge – and a maze. I would need a map to navigate my way around senior high. Zach gave my hand a reassuring squeeze. Immediately, Clive shot me an irritated look.

"Time doesn't stop for anyone," said our history teacher, Mr. Morrows. He was also our chaperone for Orientation Day. His voice echoed down the hall and our group began moving again.

"C'mon," Mia said when I hesitated. "The tour is starting again. Mr. Morrows isn't waiting any longer. He already said he had to get back to Darkmont in the afternoon."

I shrugged. Jasper would have to find us on his own. I followed my friends down the hall of our new school – well, technically it wouldn't be our school until September. This was only Orientation Day. But I still felt the way I had when I'd first started at Darkmont. I'd been sort of anxious then too. But this should be different. This time I actually had friends. Looking everywhere but in front of me, I bumped into Clive.

"Walk much?" he said sarcastically.

Ever since the flight home from Sweden, Clive and I had returned to square one. He'd finally started being nicer, but now he was worse than ever. I sighed. Even having friends brought complications. Now that I was almost fourteen, I wondered if life would ever be simple again, like it was when I was nine, my kid sister Sookie's age.

As if answering my question, Mr. Morrows guided us to our next stop on the tour: the science lab, which was really a science auditorium. There was nothing simple about this place. It was set up like a gigantic wagon wheel: the demonstration table sat in the center and the student lab tables were lined up in rows that resembled the spokes. The lab counters and tables had the cold gleam of stainless steel, and I didn't *want* to know what those sharp surgical instruments on the trays were used for. This lab was very different from Darkmont's shabby old science classroom, which only had faded animal posters and a dog-eared chart of the periodic table on the walls.

The butterflies in my stomach backflipped again. I'd let Ms. Dreeble, my science teacher, talk me into taking advanced science at senior high, but judging by this super-deluxe, high tech lab, it would be a challenge.

Jasper rejoined our group, but he didn't look nearly as bothered as Mr. Morrows that he had lagged behind. Instead, Jasper's smile was that of somebody who'd just found a new best friend.

"You should have spent longer checking out the library – it's amazing," Jasper said.

"Welcome back, Mr. Chung," Mr. Morrows said, not sounding welcoming at all. "I'm so glad you had time to join us again," he finished sarcastically.

I pushed away my worrisome thoughts and elbowed Jasper.

"Hey," I whispered. "Watch out – besides making it on Mr. Morrows's blacklist, you could lose your hard-earned jock image. Everyone will know you're secretly a geek and a bona fide bookworm. Then your reputation at senior high will be toast."

Jasper grinned, and ignoring my advice, continued. "There are more books in this library than in our town library." That was Jasper. He couldn't care less what others thought of him and somehow that made him even cooler. Go figure.

We piled out of the science lab and straggled along the endless hallways. Amarjeet was impressed with the easels and potting wheel in the art room, while Mia gushed in "oohs" and "aahs" over the big stage and greenroom in the drama studio.

"Check out the music room's speakers and take a look at those amps," Clive said admiringly, until he saw me nod in agreement. "Not like I was talking to you," he mumbled.

"No, you were talking to yourself," I snapped. I was getting tired of his constant digs. "You think you're the only interesting person in this room." Clive and I had been through a lot together – battling fairies and witches, surviving being captured by trolls. You'd think that would create a few bonds. Not that he remembered all that, but still ...

"There *are* other interesting people in this room," Clive taunted. "Just not you." Then he turned his back on me and walked away.

So much for bonds.

"Ignore him," Zach said coolly. For some reason, Zach, Darkmont School's most popular boy, had invited me to sit beside him on the plane back from Sweden. So had Clive – but how could I resist Zach, the golden boy I'd had a crush on since the beginning of school? I didn't see why that meant Clive and I couldn't get along. It's not like Zach and I were dating. Mom wouldn't allow that until I was at least sixteen. She'd made that clear. Shaking my head, I trailed behind as we headed for the lunch area.

"Whoa, check out the cafeteria. They have burgers and fries!" Mitch sounded half-starved. Our lunch counter at Darkmont only served soggy chicken fingers for the main course.

Then my steps quickened as we headed for not one, but *three* gyms. There was clearly an upside to attending a big school. Sports trophies filled a series of glass cases and the biggest trophy was awarded to the girls' soccer team.

I'd signed up for summer soccer camp and I couldn't help thinking that it might give me an edge. Maybe I'd make the tryouts of a champion team.

"Hello. Now we're talking." Zach glanced at the shining basketball court in the first gym. Cool – the doors at the back were open, and we could see that there was a track and two soccer fields outside.

"The girls and guys won't have to fight for practice time," Amarjeet exclaimed.

"You're forgetting we'll be the youngest in this school *and* lowest priority," Clive pointed out.

"Not to mention our commute time might cut into practice time," I worried. "We'll be on a bus for an hour and a half each way." Our town didn't have a high school, so we would have to travel back and forth into the city every day. Mom had suggested I could get a lot of homework done in that time, but riding on a bus always made me feel a little woozy. I'd probably only have enough energy to socialize, or maybe listen to music – especially the days I stayed late for soccer practice.

"Don't be negative, guys," said Mia. "We've been waiting to go to senior high school all our lives."

That may have been a slight exaggeration, but it *was* all we'd been talking about these past weeks. I didn't think I was being negative. I mean, I was excited, for the most part. Except ...

The students walking these halls seemed so much older. I hated the way they looked at us and smirked, like we were little kids. I'd had about enough of that when we'd visited our sister school, Svartsberg, in Sweden. Right now, at Darkmont, we were the oldest group and I liked how the younger kids looked up to us. Okay, that's weird – I hated Darkmont when I began there. Why did I suddenly feel nostalgic?

For our next stop on the tour, we visited the counselors' offices, where student guides handed out pages and pages of forms for our parents to sign. We stuffed them in our backpacks without a second glance. As we started leaving, a counselor called out – "Caitlin Peters?"

I hung back as my friends filed out of the office. "Um, it's Cat Peters."

"The register says Caitlin," she said, staring at her file and not even looking up at me. She reminded me of our vice-principal, Ms. Severn, with her short clipped hair and severely cut suit. But Ms. Severn at least looked at you when she spoke.

It's all good, I thought. It takes time to settle in at a new school. People sometimes seem cold at the beginning, but they warm up eventually – just like the teachers at Darkmont. Okay, I wouldn't go that far, but I did see other sides to Ms. Dreeble and Mr. Morrows after they volunteered to become our coaches.

"Caitlin is fine," I answered politely.

She didn't smile or glance up. Instead, she waved me into a small office. "We need to talk," she said sternly.

"I see that your shaky academic reputation has been discovered," Clive said. He had hung back too and stayed behind long enough to shoot me a spiteful grin.

I sighed.

I knew he was just being mean, but I worried he might be right.

CHAPTER 2

A Haunting Past

IT'S FUNNY HOW you're not really sure you want something until it looks as if someone is going to take it away from you. I clenched and unclenched my fists. "But my teacher recommended me," I said.

The counselor, Ms. Needlemeyer, shuffled the files on her desk. A gray folder labeled *Caitlin Peters* rested on the top. She flipped it open. "When a student is recommended for advanced placement, we have a careful look at the student's total academic standing. Citizenship and attendance are also scrutinized." She sized me up and her eyes lingered on my hair, which was streaked green. Stupid fairies had marked me and there was no dye that could cover those green streaks.

Bad news was coming. I could tell from the way the counselor used the impersonal "student" when referring to me. I wanted to protest that I'd brought my science mark up from a low C to an A over the year. Except Ms. Needlemeyer would have already seen that on my report.

Frowning, she said, "You were late a lot this past year and had unexcused absences some school days. It says you disappeared for a period of time during a student exchange. There's a note in your file that you broke into the school in Sweden after hours. A janitor had identified you in the hallway."

I hadn't realized that had gone on my record. My friends and I had snuck into Svartsberg, but only to find our teacher's daybook. Evil had been lurking on Walpurgis Night and we had to find out who was behind it. Just my luck that I was the one spotted. I'd been saving the town from a diabolical plot, which wasn't exactly an excuse adults would buy. As for the spotty attendance, well, being a fairy fighter tended to make one less punctual. Not that I could admit that either.

"Um, a few of us had forgotten our belongings and we, um, hadn't realized the school was closed."

"The file says that was your excuse." Ms. Needlemeyer scrutinized that file some more. I needed to come up with something convincing, fast.

"My teacher thinks I will benefit from the more challenging curriculum." I wasn't sure what that meant, but I figured the best way to get around the counselor was to parrot what Ms. Dreeble had explained to my mother. "So I become, ah, more organized."

Finally the counselor looked me in the eye, but only to smile that reassuring adult smile – the one they use when they want the best for you, missing the point that maybe you are the one who should decide what that is. "We like to make sure our new students are set up for success," she said. Again, she never mentioned me personally. She ran her pen across my file adding more notes.

"I can do the work," I said quietly. Even though I hadn't been sure that I could, I didn't want her deciding that for me. One thing I did know – I *could* handle a challenge.

"We don't usually allow students to take only one advanced course. We prefer students to be in one program or the other. It makes scheduling easier." She tapped her pen – code for, *I don't believe this student has the makings of a scholar.* Tap – Tap – *she's going to be trouble.* Finally, Ms. Needlemeyer said, "We will set up several prep classes for you to get ready for an entrance exam the first week of July. Then we'll revisit this based on your test score."

I shuffled out of the office as if my legs had been anchored with chains. Soccer camp was on the last week of June and the first week of July. We were planning on having so much fun. But now I would have to spend those weeks going to class, studying, and writing an exam. It would be torture. It was so ... so ...

"So have you been expelled yet?" Clive said in his most annoying, cocky way. Anger coursed through me. If I had laser vision, he would be nothing but a smoldering pile of ashes right now.

"What's wrong, Cat?" asked Amarjeet.

"I ... I ..." My voice grew raspy. Oh no – I was fighting back tears. I rubbed my hands against my eyes in surprise. Clive did a double take and his expression softened. He took a step toward me, but then backed off as if I were contagious when Zach came up from behind and put his hand on my shoulder. "Hey, what's wrong?"

I didn't want to be comforted. I choked back my unexpected tears and pasted a fake grin on my face. "I'm going to miss good old Darkmont's crowded, crappy hallways."

Everyone broke into laughter. For the rest of

Orientation, I snapped one-liners and tried to keep my mind off what the counselor had said, even though Clive kept giving me suspicious glances. Amarjeet finally pulled me aside when things had quieted down a bit. "Okay, dish it out. What's up?"

I sighed. I would have to tell them all sooner or later. "They're going to make me write an exam to take the advanced science course here," I confessed. "I might have to miss soccer camp." I had to bite my lip, but at least I wasn't sniveling anymore.

"That's not fair! Your project on wolves got the highest mark in Ms. Dreeble's class. You even won the school's science medal."

I was grateful that Amarjeet was outraged on my behalf. But I couldn't explain the rest of the bad notes in my file. She had no memory of our witch and fairy encounters – they would seem like a muddled dream to her. Only Jasper and my little sister, Sookie, would remember. Only the three of us held the white feathers that alerted us to magic. But that didn't mean *they'd* sympathize with me. Jasper was a straight-A student, so he'd just shrug and advise me to hit the books. As for Sookie – well, she was sort of in a world of her own.

"Check out your visitors, Cat," Amanda said loudly. She was another friend I'd lost since Zach and I started hanging out, especially when Zach would make room for me at their lunch table if one of the people in the popular group didn't show up. Not that I sat there the whole hour. My friends Mia and Amarjeet would have my head for dumping them. Besides, it was always awkward anyway because Clive would be glaring at me nonstop.

"Cat, I said you've got company," Amanda said even louder so I couldn't ignore her.

I looked at where she was pointing.

My mother and little sister were standing outside the main office, though I had no idea what they were doing here. Nobody's family came to Orientation Day.

Mom was beaming, while Sookie bounced with excitement. My sister's blond hair bobbed when she said, "Cat, how was your first day at the teenagers' school? Did everyone think your new outfit was cool like you'd hoped?"

A bunch of people snickered.

This morning I'd thought my new purple tunic and denim tights made me seem older – especially when I'd pulled my brown hair into a knot to show off the dangly earrings Mom had finally allowed me to wear. Well, they weren't that dangly – each earring only had two beads on a wire.

Sophisticated – yeah, right. Now I just wanted to crawl into one of those tall lockers and disappear.

CHAPTER 3

A Bad Omen

"YOUR SISTER WANTS to know if your outfit made you look cool," said Clive. His lips twisted into a wicked smile. "Don't you think you should *tell* her?"

My face heated up. Zach had taken a small step away from me, while Amanda and Emily snickered.

I just kept standing there, unable to say anything that could help me recover. I could see from the look on Mom's face that she knew I was upset. She hustled Sookie down the hall, toward the main doors. But she was too late to save my dignity. Why had Mom even come?

"Skeeter," Mom called. "It's time to go."

Skeeter?

"Hey Clive!" Clive's little brother, Skeeter, burst into the hall and came racing down, slamming into a few unwary students and sending their papers flying. Skeeter didn't stop until he practically crashed into us. He caught the look on his brother's face. "What's the matter?" he asked. Skeeter glanced at me and then at Clive again. "Are you mad at Cat again? Even though you used to like her a lot?"

Clive's expression darkened and he stormed away, which was better than what I was doing – standing around, staring helplessly at everyone's amused looks.

Mia and Amarjeet looked mortified, which made me feel even worse. I stayed frozen while my group wandered off to their next stop, until Mom came back for Skeeter.

"Sorry, Cat." Mom looked apologetic. "The younger kids have a day off, so I thought it might be fun to come into the city and take you and Mia for burgers and a movie. I brought Skeeter to keep Sookie out of your hair."

I balked. What was Mom thinking? Mia and I wouldn't want to see some stupid cartoon movie, which is the only thing Sookie and Skeeter would be allowed to watch! I replied quietly, fighting to keep the frustration out of my voice. "We're all going back to Darkmont to play some basketball. Then a *bunch* of girls are headed to Mia's for the sleepover."

"Right," Mom answered, just as quietly. "I see. I also brought you the backpack you'd packed for your sleepover. You forgot it this morning."

That would have taken me five extra minutes to fetch after we left the gym. I took my pack without saying thank you. Instead, I stared at my sneakers and tried to ignore the giggles that Amanda made sure I could hear even though she was halfway down the hall.

"Right," Mom said again. "I'm guessing you don't want a ride home."

I nodded. Maybe a few months ago it would have been fun to hang out in the city with my mom and sister, but there was no way I wanted to do that anymore. Kid stuff bored me – why couldn't she see that?

By the time Mom left, everyone had gone to visit their homeroom class, which was the last stop of the day. But I didn't feel like seeing anyone right now. I headed for the parking lot instead.

I looked for our school bus, but the lot was empty except for a super fancy bus.

"Deluxe, isn't it? It's for cross-country tours," the bus driver said as he opened the door. The smell of a brand-new car drifted out in a whoosh. "It's your lucky day."

"What do you mean?" I shook my head. Lucky day – not so much.

"This bus just rolled off the assembly line – it hasn't even been delivered officially," said the driver. "The school bus broke down, and the only thing they had available was this bus. I get to give this a test run. Hop aboard."

I stepped inside and despite my dark mood, couldn't help admiring the decor. "Cool," I said. A person could get used to traveling like this – fancy upholstery, thick carpets, televisions, reclining seats, and a washroom.

I slumped into a plush chair that even had a footstool. "Cool," I said again. I pulled on my headphones, tilted my seat back, and tuned out the world. Just as I was relaxing to the music, I heard a pounding on my window. I looked outside. Mom, Sookie, and Skeeter were staring up at me.

Mom walked to the bus door and knocked on the glass. The bus driver opened the door and let her in.

I pulled my headphones off as Mom walked down the aisle toward me. "Cat, my car engine died." She looked out the window at Skeeter and Sookie, who were chasing each other in circles. I didn't like where this was going.

"I need you to take those two back with you. There's

no way they'll last the hours it's going to take to wait for a tow truck and then wait again at the garage."

"What?" I'll admit that came out kind of harsh.

Mom pursed her lips. "You heard me."

"No," I sputtered. "I mean, can't you drop them off at the movies or something?" I looked outside again: now Sookie and Skeeter were chasing a bunch of crows around the parking lot.

"You know I can't do that," Mom replied. "I'm sorry, Cat. I'll try and make it back before the sleepover."

"It's not fair," I complained.

Mom sighed and I felt guilty because I knew she counted on me to help her out with my sister. Besides, I knew our budget was tight and Mom would have enough to worry about with the mechanic's bills. But it *wasn't* fair. "Why do I always have to be the one who has to give up on fun?"

"You're the oldest," Mom explained. "And there are times when it's not about fair – sometimes there's no other choice." She left me sitting there fuming as she herded Sookie and Skeeter onto the bus.

"Oh, Clive, I didn't see you there!" Mom said, her eyes focusing somewhere behind me.

Clive was on the bus? I hadn't even noticed him. I looked over my shoulder, and sure enough, I spotted Clive's dark curly hair several rows back.

"This is perfect," Mom said. "Skeeter can sit with his brother. The bus driver has asked that both of you keep a close eye on them – this bus is supposed to stay in mint condition." Mom winked at Clive. "You know, no chewing gum under the seats, that sort of thing."

Skeeter bounced down the aisle as if his shoes had springs and he climbed into the seat beside Clive. Clive smiled at my mom, but as soon as she left, he leaned into the aisle and glared at me. If he had laser vision, this time *I* would've turned into a haze of smoke.

"Look, Mom bought us snacks," chirped Sookie. As usual, she was completely oblivious to my bad mood. "We've got peanut butter crackers and trail mix with raisins and juice boxes and ..."

"No eating on the bus!" the driver cut in.

Sookie got that look on her face, the kind of fierce expression that meant my ride back to town would feel a whole lot longer than an hour and a half. I snatched the bags of snacks out of her hand and stuffed them into my pack.

"Hey! But Mom said ..."

"Mom says a lot of things," I said. "It's about time you learned to suffer a little as well."

Sookie looked surprised. I wasn't usually so mean, and as her eyes teared up, I almost regretted my harshness. Almost. But something cruel had dug its claws into me. "It's about time *you* made a few sacrifices," I said.

Those words felt all wrong as soon as they were out of my mouth. Then one of the crows that had been in the parking lot, the largest, blackest of them all, flew through the open bus door. Sookie shrieked as the bird flew down the aisle and headed straight for us.

It zoomed over our heads and I felt its sharp talons skim my hair. I covered Sookie's face with one arm and waved it away with the other. The bus driver scrambled out of his seat and Clive rushed toward us.

The crazed bird beat its inky wings against the inside of our window. Feathers flew and its wild caws screeched in our ears. My heart beat wildly as I leaped up to help Clive and the bus driver usher the bird outside.

Once outside, the huge black bird flew back again and banged against our window, wings flapping madly, beady eyes focused on us. Its talons scratched against the glass as if it were aiming for our faces until, finally, it flew away.

A few seconds passed while we all caught our breath. Sookie broke the silence in a hushed voice. "Isn't a bird flying into a window supposed to be bad luck?"

Chapter 4

A Dire Departure

WE HELPED THE bus driver pick up the feathers that had scattered on the ground and over the seats. "It's a good thing the upholstery's not torn up," he said. "I need some coffee. Tell anyone who comes on board to keep everything very *tidy*. I'll be back in a jiffy."

"Wouldn't want to make a mess," said Sookie, mimicking his voice. "Why does *he* get to drink something?"

I put on my headphones and turned the music louder. But even that couldn't drown out my sister's complaints. "He's probably not bringing his coffee on the bus," I said.

"Why do we even have to stay in this stupid bus?"

"It's a cool bus," I said, raising the volume even more.

"Let's just go and wait for Mom." Sookie pulled off one of my earpieces. "There's something about this bus that doesn't feel right. Something uncanny ..."

That got my attention. My little sister was sensitive to anything strange and if she felt uneasy it was good to listen. I turned off the music just as a few students stumbled onto the bus.

"Whose bright idea was it to throw an apple halfway across the room?" Amarjeet complained.

"Mitch said he was hungry and I was passing him an

apple from my lunch." Mia shrugged. "I didn't know the guys would turn it into a volleyball game."

"Now we all have to sit on the bus." Amarjeet threw herself down on a seat. "We're going to miss getting the school supply lists. And I wanted to sign up early for Art Club."

"Could be worse," Zach pointed out. "If Mr. Morrows hadn't already left for Darkmont, we'd all be getting detentions."

"There's no tomfoolery in high school," Mitch said in perfect imitation of our teacher. We all laughed, including Amarjeet. Then Mitch rubbed a small bruise below his eye. "Ow, Jasper, you really let that apple fly."

"Sorry," said Jasper, looking bashful.

The mention of Mr. Morrows made me realize our teachers would soon be part of the distant past. We would move on to a new school, where my group of friends might never have a chance to hang out like we used to. Everyone was comparing their schedule and no one had classes together. That is, everyone but me. My schedule wouldn't be decided until I wrote that stupid exam. This was definitely one of those days where I woke up thinking everything would go my way, and instead ...

"You were right, Cat. The bus driver *isn't* bringing his coffee to the bus. Looks like he spilled it all over his uniform," Sookie observed coolly. "His bag is filthy – won't that leave a stain on his new carpet?"

I ignored my sister and headed toward Jasper.

"Hey Jasper," I said, keeping my voice steady with my hard-fought resolve. "Would you be willing to help me out with a little extra test cramming? I have to take an exam to get into the advanced science program."

Jasper closed the paperback he was reading and grinned. "Sure, no problem. How much prep do you want to do – the thorough version or the abridged?"

"Full steam ahead," I said with determination. If I was going to do this, I was going to give it my all. Besides, I liked imagining the expression on Ms. Needlemeyer's face when she saw my dazzling test score.

"I can help you study." Zach craned his neck and turned to face me.

Clive snorted. "I don't think there will be any questions on baseball," he muttered, too softly for Zach to hear. I ignored Clive and said, "Any help would be appreciated." A few months ago, I would have found Zach and his shining golden hair distracting. Lately, though, I was able to think perfectly clearly when he was around.

All of a sudden the bus engine started and the driver released the brake. I had to grab the corner of Jasper's seat to keep my balance.

"Hey! Emily and the rest of the group aren't back yet." Zach jumped up and ran to the front of the bus. "I'll get them." Emily was Zach's ex. I told myself he was just being kind and making sure no one got left behind.

"The bus driver won't leave without them," Amanda answered petulantly. "Besides, Emily is talking to some older boys out in the parking lot."

But Zach was already out the door. Amanda left her seat to follow him, but as soon as she was about to jump off the bus, the driver slammed the door shut and narrowly missed squishing her.

"Hey," she said in surprise. "Could you please open the door?"

"Get back in your seat," the driver growled. Amanda opened her mouth to protest, but the bus had already lurched forward. She quickly scrambled back to her seat.

Mitch shook his head. "What's up with him?"

The bus catapulted out of the parking lot. I went flying backward, right into Clive's lap.

"Whoa," said Skeeter.

"Do you mind?" Clive grumbled.

"Quite a bit, actually." My face burned as I jumped up and into the aisle. The bus swayed as it careened down the highway. Holding on to the seats, I maneuvered my way back to Sookie.

"What about the other students?" Mia called out nervously.

The bus driver didn't answer. Mitch scratched his head "I ... I guess he's behind schedule. There ah, must be another bus for everyone else?"

I sat back down in my seat and watched telephone poles speed by in a blur. My friends chattered in the background, but Mia was still worrying that the others wouldn't have a ride home.

"If there isn't another bus, maybe my Mom can help," I said. I wasn't really sure Mom *could* help – she hadn't parked in the school lot and no one would know she was waiting on the next street for a tow truck. Still, it didn't hurt to mention that.

"The school won't leave students stranded," Amarjeet

added. "Not on Orientation Day."

"Are you sure?" asked Clive. "This is senior high now and we're supposed to take care of ourselves. My guess is that they're pooling their money to pay for a bus back to town."

"Shut up back there!" The bus driver yelled. Wow, caffeine sure didn't agree with him. We all quieted down, even Clive, out of surprise as much as to avoid annoying the driver.

"Cat, do you notice something peculiar about the bus driver?" Sookie whispered into my ear. "I don't remember his hat being so big."

The driver's hat did seem to sit farther down on his head and it was totally lopsided.

"And he's wearing jeans instead of gray pants," observed my little sister. "And dirty sneakers. He was wearing shiny black shoes before."

"Are you sure?" I thought I remembered seeing him in a spotless uniform and I hadn't notice sneakers earlier. I stood up to take a closer look.

But as soon as I did, the driver reacted. "Sit down!" he shouted.

The tone of his voice made me move back into my seat double time. That was when the bus left the city limits and turned *north*, away from the direction of our town.

CHAPTER 5

A Wicked Illusion

"HEY, I THINK you missed our turn," Mitch called out as we headed the wrong way.

"Detour," the driver snarled.

It must have been some detour because a half hour later we were *still* heading in the wrong direction. Something didn't feel right. I stared numbly out the window. My body felt frozen, but my mind was racing. There was some kind of mistake – either in my memory or with the bus driver. Sookie was right – he looked different.

I wanted to check with the others if they thought something was wrong too.

Then Skeeter shouted out, "Hey *you*, we're still going the wrong way!"

"Yeah," Mia complained. "Why haven't we turned around?"

The driver sped up and the bus lurched dangerously in and out of traffic.

"Uh, if you're in a hurry to get somewhere you could just let us out," I suggested. Not that I wanted to be stranded by a highway, but at the moment that seemed the better option.

The driver screamed, "Just shut up and let me think!"

We all stopped speaking at once, being extra-careful

not to anger the driver. But he hadn't seemed grouchy at all when I'd boarded the bus. A neat freak, perhaps, but friendly. Alarm bells rang inside my head as I struggled to find a logical explanation for the driver's weird behavior. He must have received a call to bring the fancy bus back to the depot, which must be located to the north – they didn't want a bunch of kids riding around in a brand-new bus. He just didn't feel like explaining that to us.

That was it. We were returning to the depot and we'd come back and pick up the others in a regular school bus. Of course.

Then why didn't he leave us behind, Cat?

We were in too much of a hurry, I answered myself.

But he's not the same driver, Cat.

Sure he is, he just changed his clothes.

I peered at the driver while trying to make like I wasn't looking at him at all. His jacket had grown miles too long. So, besides changing clothes he had also lost a ton of weight in a matter of minutes.

The first driver became sick and this must be his replacement.

That last thought calmed me until Skeeter shouted out, "Hey *you*, I told you we're going the wrong way!"

This time the driver lurched onto the soft shoulder of the highway and slammed the bus to a stop. Good thing none of us were standing in the aisle. The driver jumped out of his seat and yelled, "Last warning, sit still and keep your mouths shut."

"But ..."

"Quiet, Skeeter." It was the way Clive spoke to his

brother that broke the dam I'd been building to hold back the panic. The barely suppressed dread in his voice seeped into me. Then I heard Sookie sniffle.

"Cat, I ... I want to go home with Mom," she whispered. A tear crept down my little sister's cheek.

"Shh," I said, keeping my voice as steady as I could. "We'll be home soon." I unzipped my pack and a glint of silver caught my eye – I'd packed Lea's mirror to take to the sleepover. Somehow it made me feel like my fairy friend was always close. Lately I'd been missing Lea, wondering if we'd ever meet again. Touching the silver gilt around the mirror calmed me a little.

"What's that?" Sookie leaned in for a closer look. I quickly pushed the mirror deeper into my pack. I didn't want to share this memento with her. Instead I found what I'd been looking for – a package of trail mix to cheer Sookie up.

"Here," I whispered. "This won't make a mess."

We kept driving north and the bus kept speeding up. It was obvious we weren't getting home anytime soon. The more I thought about what was going on, the harder it became to concentrate.

Then I heard a rustle behind me. Clive had left his seat and was moving slowly, furtively toward the front of the bus. Jasper stood up too, ready to join him. The more the better, I thought. I signaled Mia and Mitch and in seconds we all joined them, but we either made too much noise or the bus driver saw us moving in his rearview mirror. "Stay in the back of the bus," he warned. "Or else ..."

"Or else what," Clive snapped back. We stood our

ground. That is, until the driver reached into the duffel bag at his feet.

"Or else I'll make you." The driver pulled a dark metal object out of the bag and checked over his shoulder to make sure we all saw it – a gun! I pulled Clive back and we all sat down. Sookie whimpered and I put my arm around her.

I had to face it – this bus was being hijacked and we were hostages. Strangely, this realization cleared my mind. It gave me a goal – we had to escape. Somehow. But for now, there was nothing to do but wait.

Outside, all signs of civilization had begun to disappear and the trees along the edges of the road grew dense. It was as if we were on the highway to nowhere.

"I'm feeling a little sick," Amarjeet whispered to me. Then she rushed to the back of the bus. When the driver ignored her, I came up with a plan. The bus would have to stop at *some* point, somewhere, and if a person happened to be in the washroom, and if there happened to be an emergency exit in there, that person could climb out and get help.

I waited until Amarjeet returned, looking a bit worse for wear. She slumped down into her seat. I waited a few more minutes and then I got up, gave Sookie a reassuring pat on the arm, and headed for the washroom.

As soon as I was inside the cramped cubicle, I saw there wasn't even a window, let alone an emergency exit. When I came back out, I slipped in next to Jasper instead of returning to my seat.

"Is there a way to escape?" Jasper whispered. He'd

clearly hatched the same plan as me. I shook my head. I guessed the driver must've known that, and that's why he didn't care if we stayed at the back of the bus. Skeeter piped up from behind. "What about a fire extinguisher, or anything to bonk him on the head?" That last part was muffled.

Skeeter's whisper was as quiet as he could make it, but Clive had still clamped his hand over his brother's mouth. None of us wanted to catch the driver's attention. I gave them a thumbs-down signal. Not that we should even consider Skeeter's idea. This wasn't a TV show, where kids could sneak up on someone carrying a gun and win. Someone could get hurt – badly. We had to stay under the driver's radar.

A semitruck pulled up alongside us. Its rumbling engine masked the sound of our hushed conference. "Why do you think he's taken us hostage?" I asked.

"I bet he's committed a crime or he's an escaped convict. We're insurance that he gets away," suggested Clive.

I let out a low whistle. "Well – he'll need to stop for gas eventually, won't he? Could we escape then?"

"Except that a deluxe bus like this probably has a backup fuel tank," Mitch whispered. He had snuck to the back and was sitting across the aisle from us.

"That would be, ah," Clive scratched his head, "maybe one hundred forty or even fifty gallons of fuel, if the bus had a full tank of gas."

Mitch nodded in agreement.

"This is highway driving in a mostly empty tour bus," Jasper whispered. Then he did that thing he always did when he was concentrating. He made a gesture as if he were pushing his glasses to the top of his head, even though he didn't wear glasses anymore. "I bet this bus gets about two and a half miles per gallon. So on full tanks, we could travel a few hundred miles before we run out of gas."

"If he makes it even a couple of hundred miles north, we'll be in nothing but wilderness," I sputtered.

"You're right." Clive frowned in concentration. "If this bus keeps on traveling at this rate along the highway, soon we'll have left all the towns behind. We might even make it as far as Headless Valley."

Clive was the best social studies student among us – he knew his geography – but even I'd heard of Headless Valley. That was where hikers, trappers, and miners sometimes went, never to be seen again. I gulped.

Clive continued to explain. "There's only one highway, but there are old logging roads up there, a perfect place to ditch a bus and set up some kind of rendezvous."

So not good ...

While the bus driver was busy passing the semitruck, I ducked back into my seat beside Sookie. So the big question was – how long before anyone discovered we had been taken hostage? How far could the driver travel before the police started looking for the bus? I began calculating.

Mom wouldn't be back to town for hours and she wouldn't check up on us until she returned. The other students had to somehow find their way back from the city, but then nobody would expect them back until dinner, or even later ...

How long would a parent wait before calling other parents and checking up on their kids?

That one I had experience with – maybe like an hour. But all the parents would still have to get hold of each other and then contact the staff at the senior school, and then the staff would have to check with the bus company.

This bus just rolled off the assembly line – it hasn't even been officially delivered. That's what the original bus driver had told me. And I had a bad feeling whatever had happened to him wasn't good.

There might be no record of this bus even picking us up. It could be hours before anyone tried tracking us down. And by that time ... by that time, it could be too late.

Chapter 6
A Perilous Ride

THE SKY OUTSIDE was darkening – the bus had to be coming to a stop soon, didn't it? I tried to stay awake, but after a while, the bus's lolling motion forced down my eyelids. A tap on my shoulder woke me up.

"I think we're almost there," whispered Sookie.

Almost *where*? I looked around and took stock of our surroundings. Everyone but Sookie and me was still sleeping. We must have traveled a long way – now the sky was streaked pink from the rising sun. Nights this far north were shorter than those back home, so I figured it had to be three or four in the morning. The highway was getting bumpier too. Sookie whispered that it had been a while since the bus had passed any turnoffs into other towns.

Spruce trees grew thick on each side of the road and stretched endlessly toward the horizon. We were headed for nothing but wilderness. Tree after tree flew by the window, almost making me feel seasick – as if we'd drown in this desolate forest.

The road narrowed and I spotted a logging truck heading in the opposite direction. In seconds it would pass us. When the truck pulled up alongside my window, I tried signaling to the other driver by slashing my throat and pointing to the front of the bus. Then I waved frantically. He looked up from the steering wheel and laughed. I slumped. He thought I was goofing around.

"Cat, I want off the bus now," Sookie implored.

"We all do," I whispered. "But we have to wait."

"There's great danger." Sookie looked up at me, her dark blue eyes sparkling like crystals. Her expression made her seem a lot older. "That man is a criminal and he doesn't care about us. Once he's finished with the bus, what do you think he'll do to us?"

"He'll let us go," I said as reassuringly as I could.

Sookie shook her head. "Even if he does, he'll leave us in the middle of nowhere."

My sister was probably right. Certainly some jerk that would kidnap a bunch of kids wouldn't worry what happened to them once he got away. "Everyone will figure out we've been kidnapped. They'll send helicopters to find the runaway bus."

"No one knows which direction we're headed." Sookie got that faraway look on her face – another expression I didn't much care for. It was as if she could see beyond what a normal person could even imagine. That was never good.

Sookie stared at nothing for a while. Then her eyes sparkled even more. "Cat, I think I should try and use magic. I could *hex* the driver. Make him get dizzy. I ... I think I know all the right words to the song I'd need to chant. Then we could ..."

"No," I said, cutting her off. I balked at even the suggestion of letting my kid sister use magic.

"But Cat, this man could really hurt us. He deserves

it if I put a spell on him."

Sookie had a tendency to be overdramatic. Except this time, I was worried she had it dead right. Even so, I shook my head. "Promise me you won't use a spell. I mean it, Sookie. Don't. Even. Think. About. Magic. Besides –" I thought frantically, "– if you make him sick, he'll probably end up crashing the bus and killing us all."

In my family, every second generation of sisters was faced with a choice of two fates – one would become a witch and be lost forever, and the other would become a fairy fighter, always battling dark magic. On Walpurgis Night, Sookie had drunk witches' brew from a special goblet as part of the initiation for becoming a witch. I'd saved her before she could make the deal final, but it had been a close call, and if she slipped away from me again I didn't think I'd ever get a second chance. If Sookie delved into magic – the kind of evil spell she'd need to stop this man – I'd never win her back.

"No," I repeated one more time. "You can *never* use the dark magic you've learned. Not for any reason."

Sookie gave me a searching, thoughtful look before saying, "Okay, Cat. I won't unless *you* tell me to."

"Well, that's not going to happen," I told her. Sookie just kept staring at me with that solemn, sad expression, and I shivered as if an ice cube had slid down my spine.

After a while, the bus swung off the highway, down an even bumpier logging road. I swear every bone in my body almost popped though my skin as the bus bounced along the trail. My teeth ached as they rattled together.

The landscape became more barren. Tall, craggy cliffs

rose on both sides of the bus as the road wound higher and higher toward a huge rocky plateau above. A relentless wind battered the bus, hissing through the windows in ghostly screeches.

The engine chugged and strained against the steep incline. Then a static clatter rose from inside the driver's duffel bag. The driver held on to the wheel with one hand and lowered his other arm and fished out what looked like a two-way radio. "I'm almost there. Roger."

More static. A voice responded. "Any problems? Roger."

"There was a slight glitch – someone was using the unregistered bus, but I got it back. Everything's going as planned – almost."

"Almost?" said the voice.

"Ah, roger," said the driver. "I took a few passengers along for the ride. Just in case."

"*No witnesses*. Roger that."

The driver dropped his voice, but I could still make out what he was saying. "If they can even hike their way out, it'll be a long time before they get back. Roger?"

Static. "We're landing the helicopter. Pickup is in fifteen minutes. *No* witnesses. Do you copy?"

The driver paused – maybe for only a few seconds, but it felt like forever as I held my breath.

Meanwhile, the sound of static had woken the others up. Soft snorts and murmurs rose around the bus, but died down when the others heard the snatches of conversation on the radio. It was as if a heavy shroud had cloaked all sound. Even the whine of the wind faded.

The driver finally answered. "I copy. Over and out."

I sucked in my breath. Did that mean he was going to kill us? Or did it mean that he would desert us in this forsaken place, where we might die of hypothermia, or starve before anyone found us, or get attacked by wild animals ... or ... or possibly become another grisly statistic – lost forever in Headless Valley. For a second, I reconsidered Sookie's offer. But no – I couldn't risk putting her life in jeopardy.

The driver glanced at us from over his shoulder. His face was a cold mask, but that's not where I was looking anymore. My eyes widened as he turned back around. Before I could shout a warning, a cedar bough slammed into the windshield, shattering glass over the front of the bus.

We screamed as the bus swerved and fell off an embankment.

CHAPTER 7
A Narrow Escape

THE BUS TILTED on the edge of the embankment, wobbling precariously. "Stay," I whispered as if I were talking to a dog. But this wasn't a dog: it was a forty-foot bus made of steel and glass.

The bus fell on its side with a thundering crash. I slammed against the window and Sookie slammed into me. I reached out and grabbed my sister with one hand. We both held on to our armrests as the bus began sliding again.

Metal scraped against dirt and rock, releasing a wild screech that hurt my ears. The bus, like a giant toboggan, slid several feet, and I tightened my grip on the seat and on Sookie. Our bodies pressed against the window and I could see that only a small pile of dirt and shrubs was keeping us from tumbling down. "Stay," I whispered again, stupidly.

But the weight of the bus was too much. It overturned and slid down the small embankment. Cracks spread across the glass of our window like cobwebs.

We shook around, as if we were marionettes dangling on puppet strings, until the bus hit a clump of rocks and trees, finally slamming to a halt. The jolt wrenched my arm and sent my sister and me somersaulting over the edge of our seats.

I ended up at the bottom of a giant dog pile of my friends. Someone fell on top of me, knocking the breath out of me. I couldn't have screamed if I'd wanted to. For several hideous seconds I lay gasping, trying to breathe despite the heavy weight. Black spots blotted my vision – or were those the elbows of Clive and Skeeter? I sucked in another ragged breath and pulled myself out from under everyone. Sookie was wedged between the seats.

"Are you okay?" Clive called frantically. I winced when he tugged me up by my sore arm. Shaking him off, I checked on my sister. Sookie looked whiter than Mom's freshly bleached sheets, but she managed a weak nod.

"Wow, I really thought we were gonna die," Skeeter exclaimed with some relish. Sometimes Skeeter and my sister had a warped sense of adventure. Not that Sookie looked like she was enjoying herself.

Jasper joined Clive and me, and we helped Amanda, Mitch, Mia, and Amarjeet untangle from a crumpled heap of broken glass and torn seats. Good thing everyone was in pretty good shape from playing soccer. We'd all managed to hold on to our seats. I couldn't say the same for the driver. He was sprawled out on the side of the bus – which was the floor now – and looked, as far as I could tell, unconscious. I moved forward cautiously.

"Wait," Clive said, pulling me back. I winced again. "Let's get out of this stupid bus." Clive shot the driver a dismissive nod. "He's the least of our worries."

That made sense. First things first, although that wasn't so simple considering my brain felt like scrambled eggs. I rubbed my forehead.

We all picked our way through the mess toward the window exit, which was now above us. The exit was difficult to reach, and while the others brushed glass off each other, Jasper, Clive, and I climbed on top of the tipped seats and shoved the exit door open – which didn't help my sore arm.

Jasper pulled himself up and out. He dropped on his knees and reached down while Mitch and Clive gave Sookie, then Skeeter, a boost. After that, Amarjeet and Amanda hoisted themselves out of the bus.

"C'mon, Cat," said Clive. "Your turn."

I ignored him and pushed Mia ahead of me. Mitch followed behind her.

Glancing at the unconscious driver, I felt troubled. We were far north, and even though it was June, the nights would be cold. The temperature could plunge below freezing. If that crazy driver was badly injured and went into shock, he could die. He might've threatened us, but we still had to do something to help him.

"What are you waiting for?" Clive asked, holding out a hand for me to grab.

"I think we've got to cover the driver up with ..."

"With what? We'll need our jackets and anything else to keep warm," said Clive. "It's not just about us either. We've got to think of Sookie and Skeeter too."

I knew he was right, but ... I looked again at the motionless body of the driver.

"There has to be a first aid kit," Mia said, dropping back into the bus. "It'll have a couple of those thin, insulating blankets. We could leave one on top of him."

I nodded. "Yeah, that could work." Mia's mom was a nurse and her dad a paramedic, so I figured she knew what she was talking about.

Cautiously, we made our way to the front of the bus, which wasn't easy since the floor was now the seating area. We found the first aid kit stashed beside the driver's seat. Sure enough, two foil blankets rested on the top of the kit. I spread one over the unconscious driver, and Mia grabbed his wrist and placed three fingers on it to take his pulse.

Mia's brow furrowed in concentration and she brushed back a strand of her red hair. "His pulse feels strong ... really strong." A look of uneasiness spread across Mia's face. "I ... don't think he's hurt that badly."

The radio crackled. The driver's eyelids fluttered and he moaned. Mia dropped his arm quickly and we hustled to get away as fast as we could. I grabbed the emergency pack.

The sound of Clive's voice made me jump. "I'm not leaving him with a gun," he whispered, scooping up the driver's duffel bag.

We hopped over the back of the first row of seats and rushed to the exit. My shoulder was pulsating with pain and I lagged behind Clive. Mitch pulled Mia up through the window

"Wait!" I said in a loud whisper. I ran back a few rows and scooped up my backpack. Clive was still waiting for me inside the bus when I returned. Without a word, he pushed me through the exit while Mitch pulled me out from the other side. I used my good arm to help Mitch haul Clive out.

"Wow, you're heavier than you look," complained Mitch.

"It's the duffel bag," explained Clive. "The gun's heavy."

We jumped off the bus, scrambling down the embankment. Stones and dirt scattered down the hill and rolled into my sneakers as we ran toward the edge of the dense, foreboding forest, where the others were waiting.

"What now?" asked Clive. "Do we try and make it back up to the logging road?"

"Does anyone have a cell phone?" I asked. I didn't have one – that would be a luxury on our family budget. "We could try and call for help."

Clive shook his head – I had the feeling his gran also struggled with finances.

"My parents say I don't need one," Amarjeet said with disgust. "I'm supposed to be either at school or with them. Now look."

"I'm getting one for my birthday," Amanda said.

"Not helpful," Clive snorted.

Jasper and Mitch shook their heads. I sighed. Zach had a cell phone and so did Emily. But they weren't here.

"There's probably no signal up here anyways," said Jasper. "That's why the driver and his contact were using a radio. The bigger question is – now what?" More to himself than to the rest of us, Jasper mused aloud. "If we climb back up to the road, we'll be visible from the air, which means we could be seen by a rescue helicopter, or ..."

"Or what?" Sookie demanded.

"Well, we'll most likely be seen by whoever was on

the other end of that radio." Jasper looked at me. "What do you think?"

I sighed. The real question for me was – how long would it be before help arrived? I worried that it might be a while. "The guy on the radio has a bird's eye view of the area. If we begin walking along that road, we'd be the birds – of the sitting duck variety."

Jasper nodded in agreement. "Exactly."

"Remember," I mouthed these last words to spare Skeeter and Sookie, "that guy said, 'no witnesses.'"

"That means he was supposed to kill us," Skeeter said, having no problem reading my lips. Funny, you could practically shout other words such as "Stay out of my room" and he'd pretend he hadn't heard. But this he heard easily. Skeeter shook his fist with bravado. "Ha. If he wants a piece of us, just let him try."

Ignoring his brother, Clive said, "You're not thinking this through, Cat ... We're in the middle of nowhere and it would be stupid to run blindly into the forest."

"Yeah," agreed Mitch. "I've heard of people disappearing forever inside this valley, unless their decapitated bodies uh ..." He looked at Sookie's widening eyes and stopped. "Besides, what will we eat?"

"I am thinking about it," I snapped, and then immediately felt bad. Clive was just thinking ahead, I reminded myself. He's not trying to give me a hard time. Plus this was an emergency and we had to work together. More calmly I said, "Clive and Mitch make good points, but I'm with Jasper on wanting to avoid being spotted by the criminals."

"If we can stick to the trees lining the road and keep out of sight of the bus driver and that other guy, maybe we can get picked up by a passing truck. Maybe ..." Amarjeet didn't finish the sentence. She kept glancing up at the road and then into the forest. She sounded unsure.

Not that I had a better suggestion – I didn't want to get lost in the wilderness, especially not in a forest where people were known to turn up as headless corpses. Clive nodded silently. So did Jasper.

"Okay, we'd better get moving," I said.

Before we could take a step, though, we heard the unmistakable sound of an approaching helicopter. A loud whirring filled the air and the tops of the trees around us fluttered and waved.

Our decision was made for us. We had to hide fast. But when I looked at the forest, I exchanged glances with my friends. We were all thinking the same thing.

If we entered Headless Valley, would we ever find our way out?

CHAPTER 8

Forest of Darkness

WE COULDN'T SEE the road from the bottom of the embankment. But we could see dirt fly up and branches shaking violently. The helicopter was landing. We had no other choice – we plunged into the forest.

Cedar and spruce branches slapped our faces and almost poked one of my eyes. Roots and ferns tangled with our feet. Amanda fell and Jasper pulled her up. Thorns snagged my jacket, which tore as I tugged it away. We were running downhill and it was hard to move fast without sliding. Still, I blocked all that out because we needed to get as far away as possible from the bus and the helicopter.

But if they know anything about tracking, they'll follow you, Cat. You are leaving behind a trail of broken branches and bent shrubs.

"Shut up," I told the voice in my head. "At least for now." Sometimes common sense wasn't much help.

My shoulder burned as I tugged my sister along. She'd begun to stumble, and while she was as stalwart as any kid on our soccer team, I could tell her legs were giving out. I stopped for a second and gave Sookie a chance to catch her breath. The others stopped with me and we all took a rest, panting and gasping for air.

That was when I noticed that one of us was missing.

"Where's Amanda?" I asked, surveying our group.

We all turned in circles, searching for her.

Jasper dashed into the shadows. "Wait," I called. The forest was a tangle of trees. Even if he went a short distance, he may not find his way back to us. If we kept splitting up, we would just disappear one by one.

Sookie and Skeeter slumped to the ground. Amarjeet stared nervously at the forest while Clive paced in a tight circle, his sneakers crunching dry spruce needles. He was still carrying the duffel bag he had taken from the driver. Mitch kept peering in Jasper's direction, trying to decide whether to follow him.

"No way," said Mia, grabbing Mitch's arm. "We'll just end up looking for three people."

"I'm thirsty," Skeeter said.

"Me too," complained Sookie.

I drew my hand across my mouth. I was pretty parched myself – but a couple of little juice boxes that Mom had packed wouldn't go far amongst us. "We'll find water as soon as Jasper and Amanda come back." Come to think of it, we had been running downhill. "Hey guys – remember Ms. Dreeble told us in science class that water flows downhill. Or was that in geography class, when Mr. Morrows was talking about tributaries?"

"Whatever," said Mia. "That's where water would most likely be."

"Right," I said. "We could even find a creek and follow it, instead of getting lost deeper in the forest."

"Hello?" called Jasper. I turned when I heard his voice – it was coming from the forest.

"Over here," Sookie shouted.

Jasper and Amanda crashed through bushes, toward us. Amanda was limping. "When I fell, I twisted my ankle." She gritted her teeth as her foot brushed against the ground.

"Wow," said Jasper. "I almost didn't find my way back. It all looks the same. If I hadn't heard you talking and Sookie's call, I think I would have missed this spot.

"That's why we *have* to stay together," I said with all the emphasis I could muster.

"And we have to keep our mouths shut," Clive ordered. I rolled my eyes. Clive looked at me and said, "Jasper and Amanda could hear us. So could anyone who decides to come after us."

"Point taken," I answered quietly.

"Maybe they won't come after us," Amarjeet said, also in a lower voice. "They wanted no witnesses and that's what they've got. Maybe they won't expect us to make it out of here."

"That's their mistake," Skeeter said proudly. "We're strong."

"Shh. Keep your voice down." Clive ruffled his brother's hair. "But you're right. We'll outsmart them. We'll keep moving until we find a creek and travel down it until we get rescued or find help."

Everyone agreed. Mia helped Amanda bind her ankle with a bandage from the first aid kit and then we headed out. The woods thickened as we moved downhill. It was hard going – for one thing, we were trying not to disturb the branches or the soil, so that our trail would be harder to track. The deeper into the bush we went, the more the air filled with blackflies. When they landed on me, it felt like they took a chunk out of my skin. The mosquitoes were even worse.

The lengthening shadows of the forest blocked out most of the sunlight, and the trees were so close together, we could barely see beyond a few feet. I began to have niggling doubts about our plan. What if we were traveling in circles without even knowing it? What if we couldn't find water? I reminded myself that we were still going down a slope, so we couldn't be going in circles. And wasn't there a fresh, tangy smell in the air now? I stopped for a second and listened carefully – I heard a rushing sound that had to be water.

"Let a person know if you're stopping." Clive complained when he bumped into me.

"Can you hear water?" I said. "I can't tell if it's to the left or right of us."

Amanda bent down and examined the plants on the ground. She limped ahead and I made sure she didn't wander so far I couldn't see her moving between the branches. When she called softly, we followed her until the ground grew slippery and we could see white flowers lining the forest floor. Within moments, we spotted a creek.

Huh. I looked at Amanda in surprise. She was super popular, and though she was interested in soccer, she mostly seemed to care about finding the perfect thing to wear. She never struck me as the outdoors type.

"Okay," Mia said when we reached the bank of the water. "Which direction do we want to go?"

"South," said Clive. "That's the direction the police

and search teams would be coming from. That's where the closest town would be."

I looked down and noticed that we had left clear imprints of our feet on the muddy bank. I was still worried about being followed. "But that's also the direction those guys will think we'd go," I said quietly.

"But they won't want to go back that way. That's where they were trying to get away from," Clive said.

"I guess, but do you even know which way is south?"

"Good point," Mia said, peering into the forest. Her red hair framed her face and for a second she reminded me of Red Riding Hood. She looked like she expected a wolf to jump out at any moment.

"I ... I ... think moss grows thickest on the part of the tree that faces north," Amanda said uncertainly.

Sookie piped up, "That's absolutely right."

My sister would know. She had become obsessed with gardening back in February. I tried to block that memory – she'd gotten the whole town in deep trouble with her plant potions. Instead, I walked to the closest tree. It looked like its branches were thick with moss on both sides. But the clumps of moss seemed slightly fatter on one side. I pointed downstream. "That has to be south. Let's get moving."

"Can we have a drink from the creek first, Cat? I'm really thirsty," Sookie whined.

"Ms. Dreeble told us once that unless creek water runs cold and fast, it could be dangerous to drink from." I turned to the others. "But I don't know how cold or fast it needs to be. Does anyone know?"

Everybody shook their heads, so I pulled a juice box

out of my pack. It would have to do until we figured out how to boil the water. Skeeter didn't say anything, but he stared longingly at the juice. "Why don't we take a quick break here and pool our resources," I suggested.

We all emptied our packs and pockets. Sookie and I had the most food because Mom had given us a bag of snacks and juice boxes. Mitch had nothing. Skeeter had some gum and Clive had a bag of peanuts. Mia produced a chocolate bar and Amarjeet a pack of cookies and a water bottle. Amanda also had gum.

"Bingo," Mia said, opening up a side pocket in the emergency kit. Besides bandages, disinfectant, and a blanket, there was a water filter kit, two big water bottles, and half a dozen freeze-dried packages of food.

We were going to need more than one blanket if we ended up being stuck here for the night. I regretted leaving the other blanket with the driver. He was probably sitting in a helicopter right now, stuffing his face and drinking soda. Meanwhile, we were only wearing light jackets, and now that we'd stopped running, I was feeling chilly again. I guessed it would heat up in a couple of hours when the sun reached high noon. But the nights – they'd be freezing.

"Okay, so that's not enough to keep us fed or warm," I said.

We opened a water bottle and passed it around. After taking a big gulp, I remembered something else. "Hey, Clive, what's in the driver's bag?" I took another swig of water before passing the bottle to Jasper.

A surprised look darted across Clive's face – he had forgotten he was still carrying the bag. He quickly slung it off his shoulder and opened it up.

As soon as we saw what was inside, Amarjeet gasped and Jasper dropped his water bottle.

"Jackpot!" exclaimed Skeeter.

"Oh crap," I sputtered.

CHAPTER 9

A Dicey Decision

HORRIFIED, WE GAPED at the inside of the bag that Clive had taken from the driver.

"No ..." I shook my head again.

"We are so dead," Mitch said rather unhelpfully.

"I ... I ... didn't know," Clive said, backing away from the duffel bag.

Sunlight had managed to break through the thick forest canopy. A ray struck the bag, lighting it like a blazing chandelier.

Diamonds, hundreds of diamonds, gleamed back at me. "This changes everything," I muttered.

"What do you mean this changes everything?" asked Amarjeet, her eyes not moving from the bag. Instead of looking horrified, she looked thrilled.

"Because those crooks will keep following us until they get their diamonds back," I answered in despair.

"Cat's right," agreed Jasper, shaking his head slowly. "That driver went through a lot of trouble to get those diamonds here. He hijacked the bus and took us hostage so he could be sure to make a getaway. He won't give up on them now."

"We could just leave them here," suggested Amanda. "That's what they'd be searching for – not for us."

"But what if they find us before the diamonds?" Amarjeet asked.

Good point.

"Then we'd lead them back here and show them where we left them?" Mia said, more as a question than as a suggestion.

"They'd only need one of us for that," Amarjeet countered. The diamonds were still glowing, but it felt like the world had just darkened.

"Why would they care as long as they get what they want?" objected Skeeter. "Hey, maybe we could keep a few diamonds and they won't even notice."

Sookie remained silent, but she shot me an imploring look. She still wanted me to let her use magic against the outlaws. I ignored her.

"Maybe Amanda's right," Clive said. He gave Skeeter a reproachful look. "I mean, maybe if they got their diamonds they wouldn't search for us. This forest is just as dangerous for them. But there's no guarantee."

"Yeah," I agreed. "Remember what they said about witnesses."

Clive shoved his hand into the bag and fished around. His expression grew puzzled. "I ... I ... thought the driver kept his gun in here."

"He did," I said, remembering that he'd reached inside the bag and pulled out the gray handle of a gun. Had he put the gun back in the bag? I couldn't remember.

"And what's with this?" Clive pulled out a handful of dirty pebbles. "Why are they carrying around this stuff?"

Amarjeet let out a gasp. "My uncle is a jeweler and

trust me, I've seen those before – sort of. Those aren't rocks at the bottom of the bag, they're uncut diamonds." She took the pieces Clive was holding – they filled the palm of her hand. "Look at all of them – these are worth a fortune!"

"We've got their stash and I'm thinking they won't be waiting around to get it back. Should we get going?" Amarjeet was staring anxiously at the dense trees lining the forest's edge.

"We can't go south," I said suddenly. "Those creeps will be hunting for us. They'll see the footprints by the creek and follow us."

"But if we go north, no one will find us," complained Mitch.

"Ugh," groaned Mia. "We're running out of time and it's impossible to know what we should do."

"I know what to do," Sookie whispered in my ear. "I can take care of those dreadful thieves if you let me, Cat."

"We have to head north," I said instead of replying to her. I sighed. Going in the opposite direction would fool the criminals, but the rescuers wouldn't think to search for us up there either. "We should take a branch and clear away the footprints. Then we should take off our shoes and walk along the creek bed for a while."

"But Mitch said nobody will find us if we go that way," Skeeter said.

"We can always double back," consoled Clive. "After the rescuers come and catch those guys."

"Exactly. We can always come back when it's safe," I said, even though I wasn't so sure. There might be a search party, but would they even find the bus? It had spun off the road, and if those crooks in the helicopter wanted to camouflage it, they could do that easily.

We all grabbed spruce branches, careful to use ones that had already fallen to the ground. We didn't want to disturb the trees and leave more signs. We swept our prints off the mud and then pulled off our shoes and socks and used the laces to hang them around our necks. Sookie's and Skeeter's shoes used Velcro, so I stuffed them in my pack before wading into the water.

"Mmm, that helps." Only Amanda welcomed the freezing temperature – it soothed her sprained ankle.

"The water might only be to your knees, Cat, but Skeeter and I are going to get soaked. If we don't freeze to death first." My sister crossed her arms and refused to budge until Jasper piggybacked Sookie and Clive piggybacked Skeeter. I carried the duffel bag – it *was* heavy and I was amazed Clive had been able to run with it. We kept moving forward, even as a cold ache rose from my toes to my ankles and up to my knees. But I wasn't going to complain if nobody else was.

Soon, my legs had numbed completely and I felt as if I were using stumps to walk. I think I even stubbed my toe on a rock, but felt nothing over the nagging agony of the icy water. I kept moving forward anyway.

Finally, when Jasper stumbled and almost sent both himself and Sookie into the creek, Mitch piped up. "How much farther?" he asked. He gave Jasper a break and took over piggybacking Sookie.

"We should keep moving a little longer," said Clive, though he sounded exhausted.

"Good idea," I replied, not wanting Clive to outdo me. I tried to keep my mind blank and not think of the pain as I lumbered along. Finally, we scrambled onto the muddy bank of the creek. We sent Sookie and Skeeter to fetch branches to erase our footprints while the rest of us rubbed the circulation back into our feet.

"Do you think we've gone far enough in the water to throw them off?" asked Amarjeet.

Nobody wanted to wade back into the freezing water, so after a moment's rest we started out again. We walked in the forest to avoid leaving footprints on the bank, but kept sight of the creek to make sure we didn't go in circles. After an hour or so we stopped for another break and passed around the water bottle again. Mia and Mitch went down to the creek to collect more water and pass it through the water filter in the first aid kit. When they returned, I divided up the peanut butter crackers and Mia's chocolate bar.

I let the piece of chocolate dissolve slowly on my tongue. My stomach practically leaped into my throat from hunger.

"I'll be starved to death before nightfall," Mitch said in sheer anguish.

As if in answer, my stomach growled.

"You won't starve," said Amanda. "We can eat wild plants." She reached down and pulled out a bulrush. Breaking off the fuzz, she peeled back the stalk and revealed a tender shoot. Then she dug out the bulbs. "That is, if you aren't too fussy."

Mitch stared at the bulrush for a second before

asking, "Can we at least cook it?"

"How do you know that's even edible?" asked Amarjeet.

"Trust me. I've eaten it," Amanda answered ruefully.

"Do tell," said Mitch.

"Last summer, my father took my sisters and me up to the Northwest Territories to visit my grandmother's village," explained Amanda. "It was the most boring summer of my life. My grandmother kept dragging me outside so she could teach me the Dene people's ways. Every day my sisters and I had to gather herbs and greens and cook them for dinner."

"So let's gather some of this food," said Mitch.

Amanda hung her head. "I hated it and complained all the time. But now I ... I hope I get a chance to thank my grandmother."

I patted her on the shoulder and said, "You will." Amanda lifted her head and managed a half smile. But then we both remembered we weren't exactly friends and turned away. Except that even thinking about arguing over Zach's attention seemed petty and stupid at the moment.

"So should we build a fire and start cooking?" suggested Mitch.

Clive shook his head. "We should go along for a while longer."

Though my heart sank, I agreed with him, and with a faint nod, so did Jasper. Skeeter drew himself up and offered Sookie a hand. Even though she'd been piggy-backed, dark shadows circled my sister's eyes. Skeeter seemed good to go – that didn't surprise me, since he always had energy to spare. Except –

"I'm not walking anymore until we get dinner," Skeeter demanded.

"Amanda can show us what to look for on the way so we can gather food for dinner," I said. "C'mon," I coaxed Sookie and Skeeter. "This way we can cook a feast."

"I know plenty of stuff we can cook. Nobody asked me," muttered Sookie.

We kept moving, though more and more slowly, as the shadows deepened. The warmer afternoon faded and a bitter wind rose. We could hear its shrieks as it whistled through the craggy cliffs surrounding the valley.

There was no formal agreement about when to make camp. But we all staggered to a stop when we entered a small clearing. We piled the edible leaves, rushes, berries, flowers, and roots we had found along the way onto a big rock. Even if we managed to build a fire and cook this stuff up, it would hardly be more than a salad for dinner. I wondered if there were any fish down in that creek. Maybe we could make some kind of net with the emergency blanket or with a pack.

"We're going to need some kind of shelter," said Clive. "It's getting cold."

In the distance, I heard a bone-chilling howl. Prickly shivers erupted all over my skin. Everyone stopped what they were doing and stood stalk-still.

The dreadful howl echoed across the valley and was joined by another and then another. My heart flipped and sped up.

Wolves!

CHAPTER 10

Deadly Encounters

"WE'D BETTER BUILD a shelter fast," Amarjeet said weakly, as more howls echoed across Headless Valley.

We scrambled around as we argued over how to begin. Mitch shook his head, saying, "I've never built anything without a hammer and nails before – not even a birdhouse."

"Don't look at me," said Jasper. "Woodwork wasn't my best subject." Clive muttered something about rope.

"Amanda, did your grandmother ever teach you about building shelters?" I asked.

"Not exactly. But she took me to a sweat lodge once and it was like a small shelter." Amanda frowned in concentration. "Come to think of it, they put heated stones in a pit inside the lodge, which made it really hot. Maybe we could do something like that?"

"That's a good idea," said Clive, who wasn't one to dole out compliments. "Then we can extinguish the fire and won't have to worry about smoke leaving a signal for those crooks to follow."

"No fire? Um, would that shelter hold up against wolves?" Amarjeet scanned the ragged edge of the forest, as if anticipating a wolf or a bear to crash through at any second.

"No," Amanda said flatly. "I doubt it. It's just a bunch of branches heaped up in the shape of an igloo."

"Wolves won't approach us," I said carefully. "Not if we're in a group. They would be as wary of us as we are of them." At least, that's what I remembered from my science project.

"Unless they've hunted humans before," said Amanda, who had actually spent time up north, so I figured she knew more about wolves than I did from my research.

"Man-eating wolves?" Skeeter yelped.

"That's not what I said, exactly ..." said Amanda. Then she looked at us, her eyes slightly alarmed. "The old aunties in the village would tell tales – I thought it was like the boogie man, you know, to keep us from wandering off."

"Cat," Sookie stood on her tiptoes and whispered in my ear, "maybe I should use my mag –"

"No," I cut her off. Then loudly, I said, "Let's focus on what we have to do first."

"Shelter," said Jasper.

"Heat," said Clive.

"Food," said Mitch.

Then we all launched into the work.

While Jasper, Clive, Skeeter, and Amanda set out to gather spruce and willow branches for the shelter, and Mia and Amarjeet dragged large stones up from the creek, Mitch, Sookie, and I set to work creating a fire.

We piled up all the papers from our packs that we'd received from school. I had to stop and think how Orientation had only happened yesterday, and yet it seemed forever ago – that part of my life was quickly fading into a distant memory. I shook off that thought and crumpled more papers under the kindling Mitch had laid out in the shape of a pyramid.

Try as he might, Mitch could not get the fire started by rubbing two sticks together. "This wood's too green," he said dismally. Then we tried smacking rocks together to get a spark. No luck.

"Wait," I said. "I've got an idea." I grabbed Lea's mirror from my pack and set it up to reflect the last of the sun's rays that made it through the trees. I shone the mirror onto the paper.

"It's getting too dark," said Mitch. "That's not going to work."

Then a burst of light erupted from the mirror – a strange, green light. Next thing we knew, the paper ignited and Mitch was quickly chucking pieces of wood into the fire.

"Wow, that was weird," he said cheerily as he fed the flames.

"Where'd you get that mirror, Cat?" Sookie's voice took on a strange lilt, sort of a hollow sound, like the wind blowing through the rocks. I stuffed the mirror back into my pack and mumbled, "Never mind."

"A little help here," Clive called to us. "Night's closing in fast."

Clive, Skeeter, and Jasper dumped armfuls of branches into a pile. Under Amanda's direction, we wove the willow branches in and out, building the shelter up from the ground like a snow fort. Then we covered the frame with spruce boughs. We huddled on our knees under the low shelter, scooping dirt out from the center of the floor. This was hard because we had no shovels. First we used stout sticks to loosen the dirt and then we used our hands and backpacks to scoop out the dirt and dump it outside. We took more spruce branches and scattered them loosely across the ground under the shelter. With us working together, it only took about an hour and a half – but after the day we had, it was still pretty exhausting.

"If we snuggle up like a litter of puppies, we should all be able to cram in for the night," Amanda said. "And while it doesn't exactly resemble the sweat lodge I was in, I ... I think my grandmother would be proud."

It looked like a sorry mess to me, but I wasn't about to say so. Besides, it was definitely better than nothing. Jasper and Amarjeet hauled back large, wet stones from the creek and dumped the first one on the fire. For a few seconds water spat and sizzled, until finally the stone glowed red. It was Skeeter's job to wave the smoke, dispersing it, but some still trailed up to the sky.

"How are we going to get hot stones into the shelter?" asked Amanda. "I think they used a shovel at the sweat lodge."

We mused on this until Mitch grabbed his backpack, placed it at the edge of the fire, and then used a stick to roll the stone onto the pack. "Now we can drag the rocks into the hut."

But the pack started smoldering along the way. When we rolled the stone off there was nothing underneath but a gooey plastic mess. I started coughing from the burning acrid stink.

"Whoops," said Mitch. "Guess that's not going to

work."

"Not so fast. Let's soak the packs in the creek first," I suggested. Mia and Clive volunteered their backpacks since theirs were empty anyways. We drenched them in the creek. When we rolled the first hot rocks onto the sodden pack, the pack smoked and smoldered but held together as we dragged the heated rock into the pit inside the shelter.

I sure hoped this would work. It was getting cold.

"I'm starved," complained Skeeter. "If I don't eat soon I'm going to pass out or even die."

"I hear you, man," Mitch said woefully.

We went back to the creek to gather more plants for dinner. Amanda showed us how to look for cattails and how to dig deeper into the wet soil for the long roots. "You can even eat the flowers," she said.

Mitch started gnawing on a root. "Not bad," he mumbled between bites. "Sort of like raw potato."

Sookie said that a raw potato didn't sound tasty at all. I hoped she wouldn't get stubborn. We had to eat something and there wasn't going to be any frosty oats cereal in the forest.

We gathered watercress and water lilies and we pulled out bulbs from the mud that Amanda called duck potatoes. Farther upstream we discovered more lilies from another patch of plants. The leaves were shaped like arrowheads. When Amanda pulled some out, Sookie shouted, "Stop! Those leaves are water hemlock and they're poisonous."

"What do you mean?" Color drained from Amanda's

face. "We gathered a bunch of these greens downstream. What's wrong with this patch?"

But I grabbed Amanda's hand. "Listen to Sookie. She knows about plants too." I'm not sure how much Amanda remembered about my sister's plant lore and the havoc it had caused, but she dropped the leaf. It fell into the creek where it bobbed like a toy boat before sinking.

If there's one thing my little sister knew a lot about, it was poisonous plants. Sookie had once been the apprentice of a wicked banshee named Bea, who taught her dangerous magic potions using plants from a deadly garden.

"It looks exactly the same as the other leaves," said Amarjeet slowly. "But Sookie knows this kind of stuff, doesn't she?" Amarjeet rubbed her head as if waking from a dream.

Jasper nodded. "Yeah, Sookie would know."

"There's one important difference with these plants," said Sookie in her typical, take-charge voice. But this time I wasn't irritated by her bossiness. "Their stems are tinged purple," she explained with authority. "Definitely a bad sign. Also look how all the other leaves we gathered are full of tiny holes and jagged edges from insect and animal nibbles." Then her chiming voice darkened, turning almost sinister. "Nothing has touched these leaves – not a fish, not a frog, not a bug. That's how you can tell these leaves are poisonous."

"What would have happened if we mixed those leaves in with the rest of the food?" Clive asked.

Sookie straightened up, looking livelier than she had for hours. With an almost gleeful tone, she said,

"Nasty things – even eating a little piece of root would mean a dastardly death." And then with even more relish she added, "– after you've bitten off your tongue in the throes of agony."

"Cool," said Skeeter.

Amanda paled even more. "My grandmother always checked over the plants my sisters and I gathered. I ... should have paid more attention. Sookie, could you look over the rest of the plants I found?"

Sookie practically crowed with pleasure as she sorted through the greens.

We all decided we had enough food for dinner. Amarjeet and Jasper found a large, flat stone, which they carried back and set over part of the fire. We threw all the plants we'd collected on top of the stone to cook. The plants sizzled and I couldn't believe my mouth actually began to water. Yum, bulrushes ...

Starving, we stuffed the plants down our throats – they tasted like cooked salad, only bitter and a lot chewier. Sookie grimaced, gagged a couple of times, and with an expression of utter misery, she took another mouthful. For dessert we allowed ourselves peanuts and the last of the chocolate. My stomach finally stopped growling, but the plants weren't easy to digest. While the girls tried to burp quietly, the guys started a belching contest.

We sat around the fire while the sun dropped off the horizon. Mia had snuggled next to Mitch, and I couldn't help but notice that Jasper was stealing glances at them. He'd pretty much given up hope that Mia would ever look his way instead of Mitch's.

When Jasper saw me watching, he made as if he'd been studying the skies. "We're far enough north that the sky should stay twilight instead of turning pitch black," he explained. "So we could be up all night waiting for the stars to come out."

The group broke up and Clive doused the fire. "No point taking any chances by sending a trail of smoke into the darkening sky. That would be like a flashing arrow advertising the location of our camp."

It was freezing and I hoped Amanda's plan to heat the shelter with rocks had worked. We crammed inside. Amanda was half right. The stones had heated the shelter. Even though the rocks cooled down quickly, once we all climbed into the cramped space our body heat would keep us warm. But the shelter wasn't big enough for all of us.

"In a sweat lodge you sit up," Amanda explained. "Um, I forgot we'd all be lying down."

"We should post a watch outside anyhow," Clive said. "You know, keep an eye out for any unwelcome visitors. I'll take the first watch."

"Should I go too, that way we can keep each other awake?" I suggested.

"You girls get some rest." Clive pointed to Jasper and Mitch. "The men should post guard." They nodded.

"What?" But Amarjeet's protest was halfhearted. It was warm inside the shelter and cozy too.

But I considered arguing – I hated when Clive got cocky like that, except I didn't think this was about guys against girls this time. More like, I was the last person Clive wanted to be stuck with, so instead I mumbled, "Fine."

Inside the shelter I snuggled up against Sookie. The spruce branches covering the ground kept rocks from poking our backs and made the shelter smell Christmassy. I thought about how I would rather be on watch because there was no way I could sleep – not with all my worries. Then next thing I knew, I woke up with a snort after somebody jabbed me in the ribs.

"Will you tell your sister to keep quiet and let me sleep," complained Mia.

"Huh?" I mumbled. Rubbing my eyes, I managed to make out a glint of silver inside the darkened shelter. Icy shivers erupted over my body as if I were back in that stupid creek. And it wasn't because the shelter had grown cold.

Sookie was lying flat on her stomach and staring into Lea's mirror.

"Cat," Sookie said in an ominous voice, "do you have any idea what you've got here?"

CHAPTER 11

Dangerous Magic

I YANKED LEA'S mirror out of my sister's hands. Sookie must have snuck it out of my pack while I was asleep. She often helped herself to my things. Usually that annoyed me, but it didn't usually fill me with dread. Lea was a *fairy* and fairies had magic. I could only guess the mirror Lea had left behind was unique. After all, it was a fairy object.

"Never you mind," I said once more. There was still no way I wanted Sookie to get her hands on it. I was about to stuff it in the pack, but Sookie grabbed my hand and stopped me. "Look into the mirror, Cat. Can you see?"

"See what?" This mirror had never been useful as far as mirrors go – the silver frame was beautiful, but strange too, carved with peculiar creatures that framed the glass. The glass itself had always been foggy and distorted. I only carried it around because I missed Lea. The mirror wasn't even clear enough for me to put makeup on, not that Mom would allow that yet.

I stared into the looking glass again. Even though it was dark, the mirror lit up from behind with an eerie light. I swallowed a small yelp. In the unsettling glow, it still looked like a bathroom mirror after a shower. "I can't see a thing," I said, my heart racing.

"Well I can see plenty ..." Sookie grabbed the mirror back. Then, more coyly, she added, "Interesting." I tried shaking her hand off, but her grip was tight.

"Not so fast," Sookie said. "Listen, I'm trying to tell you that I can summon help through this mirror, Cat. I'm sure of it." For a second, Sookie's small face was full of hopefulness and it tugged at my heart. Then she shifted herself on the ground so that her face was lit from underneath by the mysterious fairy light. Even though Sookie's wide blue eyes still shone with eagerness to help, under that greenish glow her face took on a foreboding appearance.

Anyone would look creepy with a light shining under their chin, I reassured myself. Except I knew Sookie wasn't just anyone. Once more I snatched the mirror away. "Rescuers are coming at any moment," I reassured her. "We don't need any help from a fairy object."

It was a hollow promise. I had no idea if the runaway bus had been discovered. Nor was I sure using this fairy object would be a bad thing. After all, Lea gave it to me and it had helped me before. Also I carried a feather that was from Fairy, and it helped me remember the twisted enchantments that befell our town, even when my friends didn't.

I hesitated. The glint in my sister's eye worried me. Sookie was on the edge – ready to tip from our world into a world filled with evil magic – *maleficium*. Witch blood ran in our family, and so far, my sister had come pretty close to becoming a full-fledged witch. That seemed a lot more dangerous than spending another night in the forest waiting for the police to find us.

"Please let me use the mirror. I can help," Sookie begged.

"No."

"Don't boss me around," Sookie burst out. "You don't know everything. I knew what plants we could eat – but you never asked. I can stop those outlaws, but you won't let me. You're not Mom." Sookie choked up as soon as she mentioned our mother.

"Do you two *ever* sleep?" Mia grumbled as she rolled over and faced us. Mia had been our roommate in Sweden and I knew from previous experience she was a light sleeper and couldn't stand noise. Even though the shelter was dark, the mirror's green light swirled and spilled out of the glass, illuminating the inside of the shelter with a ghostly glow. Mia didn't seem to notice this, but there was enough light for me to see her shake her head in disgust.

"Seriously," Mia hissed. "Sleep or don't sleep. But be quiet." A few of the others snorted or groaned after she rolled over and turned away from us.

Finally I wrestled the mirror away from Sookie. I'd been using my backpack as a pillow and Sookie must have opened the zipper without waking me. I stuffed the mirror back inside the pack. "Get some sleep," I ordered Sookie before I crawled out of the hut.

"Need a break?" I asked the guys.

"I'm out of here," Mitch yawned.

"There's actually room for one more person inside – if you sit. It's definitely warmer." That was good enough for Jasper. He followed Mitch. It was cold outside the shelter. The good news was that this meant no mosquitoes. The bad news – Clive and I would have to huddle up close under the one emergency blanket – none too easy when you weren't feeling too friendly toward each other. But I didn't want to go back and keep arguing with Sookie. Mia would kill me.

Clive frowned.

I sighed. "I'm staying outside. You can go back inside, if you want. And you can get Amarjeet or Amanda to come out – if you don't think I can handle it," I added a little sarcastically. "I don't care either way." I yawned.

Clive yawned as well. "We probably should keep each other awake," he said, seemingly too tired to snap back with a mean reply. When I sat beside him he became as silent as a stone.

He'd moved closer to the last remnants of the fire, trying to soak up more heat. I slipped under the blanket, pulling my knees up to my chest and wrapping my arms around my shoulders for more warmth. Sitting in silence in the middle of a wild forest at night, wondering if you'll ever make it home in one piece, weighs on a person's mind. I really wanted to plan things out with Clive, to get his take on things. He wasn't the easiest person to get along with, but he was brave, and this I had to force myself to admit, smart. Just a few short weeks ago, I thought we'd become friends – but that had all changed. I wanted to ask him what went wrong and was about to when a wolf howled.

Its haunting call hung on the air, sending prickly feelings up and down my skin, as if I had walked through cobwebs. I shivered.

Another wolf howled, and Clive said, "Tell me what

you know about wolves."

"They're not supposed to be that dangerous to humans," I answered shakily. At the moment, though, I was thinking that reading about wolves was one thing. Hearing them howl in the middle of the night in a forest was a whole other thing entirely. Besides, when I listened to their howls on YouTube, it sounded nothing like these menacing wails.

"What do you mean by, '*that* dangerous,'" Clive pressed, picking up on my worried vibes.

"They're not usually aggressive – unless they're sick or really hungry. Or ..."

"Or what?" asked Clive.

"If wolves were in a big enough pack, they'd be more courageous, though cautious. There's no way they'd attack right away except ..."

"Except what?"

"They're intelligent. They've been known to stalk their prey to figure out a plan of attack."

"Right," Clive said. "So ... we should be okay in camp tonight." He said that as if our only hope was to get out of here fast. I was forced to admit he was right.

Another howl ripped through the woods. Then quite a different sound echoed throughout the forest – the snapping and breaking of branches.

A thin creek of light bobbed in the distance, threading through the trees – a flashlight.

We weren't alone.

CHAPTER 12
A Diabolical Plot

WORDLESSLY, CLIVE AND I made hand signals to one another. Then I climbed back in the shelter and woke Jasper, who'd somehow managed to fall asleep sitting up. He didn't exactly appreciate me clasping my hand over his mouth, but I wanted to make sure he didn't make a sound. As his eyes opened, I whispered in his ear, "There's someone coming." Jasper's eyes grew even wider.

"Wake everyone quietly," I whispered. "Then disappear into the forest and head for the creek. Clive and I will meet up with all of you farther upstream."

When we got back outside, Clive and I dived into the forest to spy on the visitors. First we looped behind to where we had heard the snapping branches. Between copses of trees, in the deepest shadows of gloom, we spotted two men. My heartbeat raced. One of them was the bus driver and he was limping.

"My head's splitting," the driver said. "There's no point searching around here in the night. I'm gonna trip on a stone and break my leg." He stopped and leaned against the sweeping branches of a fir tree as he caught his breath.

"That'll match your cracked skull," said the other guy in none too sympathetic a voice. "This is where we thought we saw smoke, this is where we search. We find the diamonds, we take care of the witnesses, and *then* we hike back to camp."

Take care of the witnesses – I gulped. That voice belonged to the pilot we'd heard speaking over the radio.

"I didn't sign on to kill a bunch of kids," said the driver.

There was a slight hiss beside me as Clive let out his breath. Even when you imagine the worst, you don't actually believe it until it stares you in the face – or, in this case, until you hear it straight up. But the bus driver didn't want to kill anyone. My heart warmed to him – a little. Then he stubbed his sore foot on a twisted root and let out a stream of bloodcurdling curses, mostly targeting "idiot kids."

"They've got eyes, so they'll look in the bag," his companion growled. "And they've got mouths, so they'll tell someone about the diamonds. How can we keep it secret now, tell me that?" He waited a few seconds and when the driver said nothing, he continued to rant. "We're talking multimillion dollar deals here. We have investors from all over the world. They think they're buying into diamond mines because we brought those diamonds up here for them to find. After all these years it's almost a done deal. We can't have witnesses screwing it up."

Clive and I drew back. We looked at each other with panicked expressions. "We're in deep," he whispered, shaking his head. "These guys are going to use the uncut diamonds to salt the mines. They're going to trick investors into thinking there are diamonds up here!"

Clive may know a lot about geography, but I was good at math. I could add. *One* – they were bringing uncut diamonds up north to scatter in old mines to fool people – *plus one* – they were going to sell lots of stocks in diamond mines. That equaled *two* bone-chilling facts – they had to keep their scheme secret and that meant they had to get rid of us.

"Anyone who knows the truth about those diamonds can't be allowed to live," I said with a sinking heart. The expression on Clive's face showed that he'd reached the same conclusion.

"We gotta take care of loose ends," the helicopter guy finished. They stayed huddled under a tree while they argued. This guy never used the word "kids" like the driver had. To him, we were obstacles, nothing else. I shuddered.

"But there's nine of 'em, and two of them are little," the driver whined, but with less confidence.

"Yeah, well you're the one who decided to drive away with a busload. You could have just kept one or two as hostages," said the pilot. They started out again.

Blood rushed to my head and it felt as if there were no other sounds in the forest – not the snapping of branches as the bus driver and the pilot pushed through brambles, nor the ragged wail of the thin wind that blew constantly through this valley – only the echo of the outlaws' voices.

"They'll be dead out here in another day or so. What's the hurry," the driver argued. "Let nature do the dirty work."

My heart cooled toward him. How could he think if we starved to death or got killed by wild animals that there wouldn't be blood on his hands? I shook my head in disgust.

"We don't want to stay here any longer than we have to. This valley has a way of turning on everyone," warned his companion. "Even expert trackers disappear or lose their heads. We get the job done and get out as fast as we can."

A string of wolf wails froze my blood – it had the same effect on those crooks. They stopped in their tracks.

"That's it," the driver rubbed his head vigorously. "We've almost found them, and those kids aren't going anywhere for a while. We'll go back to camp and find them when it's brighter. They're just kids and they've had no food. They're probably freezing and crying for their mothers right now. They'll be in bad condition and won't get far."

The pilot nodded as he pulled a long, dark object – a rifle – off his shoulder, checked it, and sighted it.

I turned to head for the creek, but Clive grabbed my shoulder and pointed in their direction. I knew he wanted us to follow them and find out where they'd camped, but I didn't want to leave our hiding spot. It wasn't pitch black, but the trees were densely packed and everything looked the same in the gray twilight – how would we find our way back? *Yeah, right – if the wolves don't find you first.*

The problem was I knew too much about wolves. I understood that a group of kids at camp were safer than a couple of kids stumbling around on the wolves' turf.

Then I thought about Sookie and Skeeter, and how those men were willing to let them die. I decided I'd take my chances with the wolves.

I kept up with Clive as we crept behind the men, all the while conserving my energy like I would on the soccer field until time for a breakaway. The smell of rotting leaves and stumps grew thick in the air, clinging to my tongue like a bad taste, and it was getting harder to detect the sharp tang of water from the creek. I didn't want to lose direction.

As we followed, our feet started bouncing off the ground as if we were on a cushiony turf. It was easy to travel and easy staying deadly silent. Then I shoved my foot into some tall grass and sank in mud and icy water up to my knee. I let out a tiny yelp and then bit my lip, hoping the men hadn't heard. Clive turned as my leg made a sucking sound when I yanked it out. We were in a bog.

My sneaker sloshed as we backtracked away from the bog. It was easy to stalk the men. They were confident of their strength and of our weakness, so they didn't even try to keep quiet or to watch where their flashlights shone. I could have followed them with my eyes closed, except for the bog part. Anyway, we weren't a bunch of weak and scared kids like they thought. We were surviving just fine. A doubt formed in my head like a warning whisper. *You can't survive out here forever, Cat.*

A couple of minutes later, Clive and I peered through the trees as the men walked into their camp. The slight edge I thought we had disappeared. They were confident for a reason. They had the best equipment – a fancy tent, Bunsen stove, top of the line gear stacked to one side, and crates of food. They had compasses and satellite navigators, Gore-tex coats, and thick hiking boots.

As I started calculating our chances, one more guy came out of the tent – a big, bald, muscle-bound thug. I pictured all of us trying to tackle him and him shaking us off as if we were annoying kittens.

Three of them pitted against nine of us. Except they were expert woodsmen and they had guns. Clive paled. I figured he'd come to the same conclusion I had come to.

Situation: hopeless.

We stole away. Clive wasn't a bad tracker himself. We found our way back and realized we hadn't traveled far – only our fear had made it seem that way. Those men were dangerously close to us. Jasper had managed to get everyone out from the shelter, so Clive and I made our way to the creek.

"You know, um," Clive began saying. "Unless a rescue comes today, I don't think, um ..."

"We will last until tomorrow." My voice went flat. Clive shot me a strange look – half despair and I think half admiration. I was willing to face the truth, which he could lay out without worrying about me fainting or crying or something. He was such a ... guy. I winced. The problem was Clive didn't know I was facing a much harder decision.

"You made it," Amarjeet said in relief. We'd found our friends upstream, grouped at the rocky bed of the rushing creek. "What's the scoop?"

"It's not good," I said.

"Yeah, those wolves got close," Mia said. "They sounded ..."

"Like they were going to try and eat me," said Skeeter, shaking his head.

"The wolves are gone," Clive reassured his brother.

"Oh, I wasn't scared," Skeeter said. "If they come

back I'll take a branch like this, see?" He reached down and grabbed a forked branch and jabbed it fiercely into the air, forcing us to scatter. "I'll hit them with this stick right between the eyes and those wolves will run away."

Amarjeet stared at Clive's drawn face as he watched his brother battle invisible beasts. "We've got more to worry about than wolves," she said quietly.

I nodded mournfully.

"What?" asked Mitch. "I'm missing something here." Jasper glanced nervously upstream. Amanda had taken off her shoe and was soaking her sore ankle in the water again.

Sookie stepped forward and crossed her arms. She waited.

"Those creeps are closing in on us, and they're not going to give up," Clive said bluntly.

"Then I'll just do this," bragged Skeeter, jabbing the stick again.

"I'm afraid that won't be much use against guns," said Clive. Then he tried a half smile. "Though I'm glad you're on our side."

"I'm on your side," Sookie said to me, still waiting.

"All right," I said louder than I meant to. Everyone turned. "Okay, Sookie. You can help."

CHAPTER 13

A Treacherous Choice

I FELT AS if we were all hanging on to the edge of a cliff by our fingernails – and my sister had the rope that could save us. That was the only reason I'd just told Sookie she could use a tiny bit of magic to help us. I hoped I had made the right choice, but it didn't help that Sookie squealed with glee.

The rest of the gang didn't appear as ecstatic. "What can *she* do?" Clive asked suspiciously.

"Use the mirror to summon help!" yelled Sookie with too much enthusiasm.

"Calm down," I shushed her. "I just want you to ..."

"Give it to me, Cat."

I didn't like the way Sookie's face lit up when she talked about the mirror – as if there were more going on than her wanting to get home. More like, she couldn't get the fairy object out of her mind. I had a bad feeling ...

"Maybe we should wait," I said, backpedaling. "Help is close. The police must have discovered the abandoned bus by now." By the look on their faces, I could tell Clive and Jasper weren't so sure.

"Your sister can call for help? I thought none of us had a cell phone," said Mitch. "What's she waiting for, I can't live off of duckweeds for dinner much longer."

The early light was breaking through, warming up the morning air. A faint buzz told me it would only be seconds before the mosquitoes began to harass us. Even just the sound of the pesky bugs made me want to scratch my arm.

"Your sister's not talking about a cell phone ... is she ...?" Amarjeet said slowly, as if she were trying to dig up a buried memory. "Sookie's not like other kids."

Mia stopped flicking stones in the creek and turned. Her face grew puzzled. Then Skeeter piped up. "Cool. Sookie, are you going to use some magic? Let's get those bad guys."

"Magic?" Clive's eyes bored into me. "Why does this seem familiar?" Then he shook his head. "Why does even saying, 'this seems familiar' uh, seem familiar." Mia nodded in agreement.

"Because it is," Jasper broke in. "Sookie has special talents, and weird things have happened before to all of us." He didn't go on to explain that only he and I remembered this because of our white feathers – the feather I kept on a fine silver chain linked around my waist – the feather that at this very moment heated against my skin in warning. As if I had a choice ...

The eerie howls of wolves echoed across the valley. That was weird – they should have gone back to their den by now, even if they were traveling in a pack. Something about their howls disturbed me – aside from hearing a wolf in the first place. I couldn't quite put my finger on it.

"Those guys at the camp aren't going to like the wolf cries either," Clive said. Then more urgently, "They are going to want to get their diamonds and get out of this valley fast."

I got his point: that meant those guys would be in a hurry to get rid of us, and judging from my friends' wounded expressions, they understood that too. Skeeter thought this was a stupid game or adventure, like in the movies, and Sookie – well, at the moment she seemed preoccupied. Her hand was still stuck out, waiting for me to hand over the mirror. Maybe she wanted this just a little too much.

Skeeter leaned over and began chanting loudly, "Use your magic. Get those bad guys."

Clive huddled with the others and updated them about the diamonds as well as the driver and pilot's plan. I felt a sense of foreboding tighten around me like a noose. Clive was right – those crooks would find us in an hour or so tops, if the wolves didn't find us first. Suddenly I knew what had made me uneasy. The howls reminded me of a spy show I'd watched on television, where the spies used Morse code. Those yowls sounded eerily like signals. The pack was closing in, but I hadn't read *anything* about wolves knowing how to communicate like that. I was beginning to think there was a reason those howls sounded different. There was something uncanny in the air – I could feel it.

Clive broke away from the group. "Even though I should be saying this is all a load of crap, I ... I won't." Clive looked pained to admit it. "If there's some way your sister can help us, now would be a good time."

"Fine," I answered, almost in defeat. I couldn't see

another way out. Then I held Sookie's gaze with mine. With a sigh, I said, "If there's some way you can get help with your magic, then let's do it." My sister nodded enthusiastically. I reached in my pack and pulled out my mirror. Everyone crowded around me, and Amanda gasped at its strange light. Reluctantly, I handed it over to my sister. She yanked it from my hand greedily.

"Uh, is it just me or do you think we should, like, get moving rather than stand around staring at some mirror?" said Mitch.

"It is going to take a while," said Sookie. "Mirror magic doesn't just happen. It needs to be lunar charged."

"Right ..." I said slowly. Like we had time to wait until the moon came out. Nothing came easy – not in our world or the magic world. But it hadn't occurred to me that this wouldn't happen instantly.

"Besides moonlight," Sookie explained, "we'll need to find a place of power." Then, as if I were the little sister, she started lecturing me. "Those are earthly points that are linked to the Otherworld."

I stared blankly.

"You know," Sookie said, slightly exasperated. "Like Grim Hill or Blakulla in Sweden."

"Oh," Amarjeet said quietly as if it were all coming together. "Places where strange things happen ..."

Mia grew thoughtful, mumbling, "My grandfather used to say something about places like that. He called them *ley lines* ..."

Amanda nodded. "The Dene and lots of First Nations people have places like that. I saw one once when I was with my grandmother."

I was about to ask what it looked like because in my experience, getting to a place of power usually involved climbing hills or mountains. That didn't seem possible, trapped as we were between the wolves and the outlaws.

"Did you hear a branch snap?" Mitch stared wildly at the bushes ahead. "Let's get out of here." He turned to Sookie. "Can you buy us some time while you figure out what to do with that mirror?" Already my friends were looking to my kid sister, letting her take charge.

"I can use a foot-track reversal spell to throw those desperados off our trail," offered Sookie.

"Why didn't you do that yesterday," Clive complained. "They wouldn't be on our backs now. Not to mention it would have saved us a trek through the icy creek."

"Cat wouldn't let me," Sookie said in disgust. Then, apologetically, she looked up at me and said in her sweetest voice, "Don't worry. I'll conjure just a little *hex*."

Hex. The cat was out of the bag and it wasn't me. My sister was unleashing her powers.

CHAPTER 14
Dead Lost

"QUICK," ORDERED SOOKIE. "Hand me something that belonged to those unscrupulous outlaws."

"Huh?" asked Mitch.

That was my sister – all about the drama. I sighed. "She wants a diamond."

Clive slung the duffel bag off his shoulder and opened it up. He hesitated for a second.

"Come on," Sookie said with a hint of impatience. "If it's a shiny object it will work even better – it will distract them like a flashy bauble would distract a magpie."

"What's a magpie?" asked Mitch.

"Could we just get this over with?" I said. Clive snatched a diamond out of the duffel bag and handed it to my sister.

The moment would have been very funny, if I weren't so busy fearing for my life and for my sister's fate. To see Sookie boss Clive around, and have him obey, brought back memories of him lecturing his brother about doing whatever Sookie told him. Then, Skeeter began chanting again.

"Use your magic, get those bad guys."

It was eerie, as if he too were falling under the magic's lure.

This is the right thing to do, Cat, I repeated to myself.

This is the only way.

Sookie gathered dirt from each of our footprints left in the muddy silt and sprinkled it over the diamond. Her voice grew ominous as she pronounced, "Bow la." That's what it sounded like, but I knew my sister was saying, "*Bear leat,*" which is Celtic for "take this away."

Sookie began singing her own peculiar song, which I swear was one of those creepy tunes she'd learned from the evil witches in Sweden. I gulped. Sookie flashed a wicked smile before she looked up at me and dropped her grin. Suddenly a murder of crows erupted from the trees and flew into the air, cawing and screeching. I followed the flock with my eyes and spotted a strange sight that froze the breath in my lungs.

"Wow," said Amarjeet. "I've never seen anything like that."

"What ... what was that?" asked Mia.

I couldn't take my eyes off the strange bird with its cream-colored feathers and arched wings spread like ivory fans.

"A white raven," Amanda gasped. "Some First Nations people say a white raven is a harbinger of the end of the world."

"Harber what?" asked Mitch, his eyes riveted on the sky.

"Harbinger – a sign of something bad to come," said Jasper. "I can't believe seeing an amazing creature like that would be a bad sign."

Amarjeet shook her head. "In my culture, if something appears in white, it means it could be a ghost."

"Bad sign, good sign, we have to stay focused," Clive broke in. "Our lives are in danger. Let's get moving."

"There's no rush," Sookie said coyly.

"Why? What did you do?" asked Clive.

"Sookie kicked their butts." Skeeter grinned.

"Those men won't see our footprints," said Sookie. "And they'll keep on circling back the way they came – for a very long time." Then my sister suppressed a giggle. "Oh, and their feet are going to get a terrible rash that will make their skin horribly itchy."

"Awesome," Skeeter said with approval.

"Clive still has a point," said Jasper. "We need to escape while we can. Those guys won't keep circling forever." Then he fastened Sookie with a serious stare. "Will they?"

Sookie shook her head. "Not ... forever ..."

We dived into the sea of trees and hiked deeper into the valley. But we'd had little food and sleep, and soon we began stumbling over the twisted roots that spread across the ground. It was almost as if those trees were tripping us on purpose.

"I can't take another step until I get something to eat." Skeeter sank to his knees.

"Should we take a break?" I said, and before I'd even finished my sentence, Amarjeet, Mitch, and Sookie slumped to the ground. Even Clive didn't object. We passed around the last of Mom's snacks, sharing peanut butter crackers and apple juice.

"Ouch." I slapped a red bump forming on my neck. In the shadowy gloom of the forest we were becoming breakfast to a steady onslaught of mosquitoes.

Batting away the bugs, Mia asked, "If those guys are looping from the creek back to their camp, can't we head back to the road?"

"What if we cross paths with the driver and his nasty friends as they are circling – we just got rid of them," grumbled Clive.

We slowly pulled ourselves up from the damp ground. I wasn't happy about plunging deeper into this forest.

"Hey," said Mitch. "But if we could hike back to the bus, then we could *use the radio* to get help while those crooks are under Sookie's spell."

"Whoa, now you're talking," Clive said.

I liked that plan too – then my sister wouldn't have to use her hocus pocus on that mirror.

"Good idea, Mitch," said Jasper.

"Hello, I was the one who came up with the idea," Mia shook her head. Amarjeet nodded in agreement.

"No, you didn't," argued Mitch. "You didn't mention the bus or the radio."

"I said we should hike back to the ..." began Mia.

We all started arguing until Jasper said, "Hey, does anyone have any idea which way the bus would be?"

I looked around in the gloom. This place seemed different from the creek path we'd followed. The ground had grown springy again, and I didn't like the way the air smelled – like toadstools and rotting stumps and dark secret things.

"Remember," began Amanda. "Moss grows thickest on the north side of trees. That's the way we headed, so we should turn around and go south."

"Uh, that moss stuff is not going to help," said Amarjeet.

She was right. In this stretch of the forest, moss hung like beards on stooped and twisted trees. It was impossible to tell on which side of the tree it grew thicker. Not only did this seem like a place where you'd find Red Riding Hood, it reminded me of the dark and dangerous forest that Hansel and Gretel had stumbled into. I used to think those were simply fairy tales, until I began living under a fairy hill.

One glance at Jasper and Clive's faces forced me to admit the truth.

We were dead lost.

CHAPTER 15

A Sinister Turn

"WE HAVE TO pick a direction fast," I said. "It'll be getting cold soon." The wind seemed to agree with me – it blew through the crags of the surrounding rocks in shrill, urgent gasps.

"I think the creek's this way," Mia pointed right. "If we could follow it, we'd get back to ..."

"I'm pretty sure it's the other way," said Mitch.

Half of us thought the creek was to the left, the other half believed it was to the right. "Maybe the mirror would help," Sookie suggested.

"It's not a compass," Clive shot back impatiently.

"We don't know what that mirror is," I said slowly. I dug it out of my pack and handed it to my sister. I told myself that fairy object or not, the mirror had belonged to Lea and couldn't bring us harm. Sookie grasped the gilt edge, her knuckles turning white as she scrunched her eyes and stared into its foggy glass.

"We should turn left," Sookie said. No one argued this time.

* * *

Blackflies plagued us as we plowed our way through

endless trees and bushes. After a long time, we stopped to pass around the water container. It was hard not to gulp it all down at once, but we didn't dare finish it off until we found the creek again. Everyone had glum expressions and even Sookie, as excited as she was, began stumbling with exhaustion.

"This is taking longer than we'd planned," Mitch pointed out. "Why don't we gather some more plants to eat?" We all agreed, and even the thought of bitter leaves made my mouth water as my stomach practically gnawed through my spine.

The air began turning cold, which got rid of the flies, and the shadows grew long in the dimming forest light. We set out again, gathering edible plants and berries on the way.

"Oh no," Amarjeet cried out in utter despair. "We're going in circles."

"What do you mean?" Clive looked around. "We haven't been here before."

Everywhere looked the same to me. I shrugged my shoulders.

"Check that out," Amarjeet pointed to a bush of salmon berries. "I remember breaking off those branches to get to the berries."

Amarjeet was right. I could make out our footprints in the dirt. I blinked back tears as I tried not to think about how tired, hungry, and frightened I was becoming.

"Good one, Sookie," Amanda complained. "We're not getting anywhere."

Sookie crossed her arms and stubbornly said, "The mirror meant for us to go left."

"I knew we should have gone right," said Mia. "No one ever listens to me."

"It doesn't make any difference," Jasper pointed out. "We're traveling in circles – so what if we're circling left or circling right?"

"Like I said, that mirror's no compass," argued Clive.

Sookie's lip quivered. "I shouldn't have given the mirror back to you," she said looking up at me. "I should have kept checking it while we were hiking. Oh, Cat," she sniffled. "I want to go home."

Slapping a smile on my face, I ruffled her hair and promised, "Soon." I grabbed the mirror from my pack and handed it to my sister. "I guess it's okay to look one more time."

Once more, Sookie pointed left. With no other choice, we set out again, grumbling and sniping at each other as we trudged in exhausted misery, until ...

"Awooooo." The shuddering howl ripped through the trees and froze our blood. It was almost as loud as a clap of thunder.

"Awooooo."

Those howls sounded closer than ever before! For cover, we dove deeper into the trees and broke into a panicked run. Trees and branches bit my skin and snatched at my hair. I was gripping my sister's hand. When she tripped, I wrenched my shoulder again. I noticed the ground below my racing feet was springy. At least this time I knew to watch out for the tall, reedy grass. "We're headed into a bog," I warned them. We backed away and, panting, stopped our crazed run to catch our breath.

"What's that over there?" Jasper pointed to a small clearing.

A large silhouette appeared in the shadows. Could it be possible? Had we really stumbled upon a cabin in these woods? Another howl tore through the trees and we all began running toward it.

This wasn't the gingerbread house from Hansel and Gretel – there wouldn't be any witches.

I peered down at the blond head running beside me.

At least, that's what I hoped.

CHAPTER 16

A Foreboding Discovery

A SKELETAL TREE stood outside the dilapidated cabin. One branch's long twig fingers tapped a haunting rhythm against the grime-covered window. Another branch swayed in the wind, beckoning us inside with its ghostly wave.

"This place looks haunted." Skeeter slowed his approach.

We all slid to a stop outside the cabin's darkened door, not enthusiastic about entering, not daring to remain outdoors while the wolves howled. Surely, inside would be safer. I reached out and grabbed an old-fashioned handle made of twisted iron.

"It's locked," I said.

"Are you sure?" Clive tried the latch, and while the handle rattled, the door didn't give. "It's stuck," he said. "Mitch, Jasper, help me push."

The three of them heaved the door, and though Clive didn't think to include us, Amarjeet, Mia, and I began kicking the wood. It finally creaked open with a scratching groan, which was every bit as horrible as the sound chalk makes when it screeches down the blackboard.

"Uh, ladies first?" Clive peered cautiously inside the cabin.

"Glad I'm not a lady," I shot back, even though I knew he was joking. We stepped inside the cabin together.

An old rusty wood stove stood in one corner of a large room. Beside the stove was a tottering wooden table surrounded by three chairs, all with broken slats. The table was set with a plate, mug, knife, and fork. The mug and plate were probably white once, but the grunge of undisturbed years had turned the enamel a dingy gray.

An iron bed was shoved against a wall and its tattered quilt had disintegrated over time. The pine board floor was coated with an inch of dust. My allergies kicked in and I let out a sneeze.

"*Gesundheit*," Clive said automatically.

Rickety winding stairs led up to a loft, but it was too dark to see what was up there. Gingerly, Clive and I stepped inside, as the others followed. I let out another sneeze. Old has a smell: musty and corrupt. This place stank of something ancient.

"Whoever lived here sure left in a hurry," Clive said, pushing ahead of me and lifting an old-fashioned coffee pot from the stove.

The bottom of the pot had burnt through and ashes scattered over the stove as soon as Clive moved it. Someone had planned to drink a nice cup of coffee, but never got the chance to pour it. For some reason, this made me shudder.

Toward the back of the cabin there was a large window, but it was covered with gray, ragged curtains that hung like cobwebs. For a second I wondered why anyone needed curtains – the place was in the middle of a forest where there was hardly any sunlight ...

"What if we stay here," Amanda said. "We could clean up a little. If we could light a fire in the stove, we'd be set for the night."

"And maybe rescuers will spot this place or maybe they already know about this cabin in the woods and they'll look for us here," Mia added hopefully.

It didn't look like anyone knew about the place to me. Clearly nobody had stepped inside for years. "We can't be that far from the road," I said halfheartedly. I still liked the idea of finding the bus and using the radio to call for help.

Everyone quickly shot that notion down. They were right – I don't know what got into me. Night was settling in, wolves were lurking nearby, and we were utterly lost. We couldn't leave now.

Then, in a quiet voice, Sookie said, "I don't think this is a very good idea."

"What's with you two," Clive said in disgust. Then he said to my sister, "C'mon. The cabin will look great once we men build a fire and you girls cook the food and clean up a little."

"How come you are men and we are girls," I said.

"And she's back," Amarjeet added with a smile.

"You don't like being called a girl or a lady. Are you ever satisfied?" Clive got that cocky expression that drove me crazy. "Fine, the guys light the fire and ..."

"Men, guys, who cares – don't think you're not cleaning up," I added.

"You've got that right," said Mia.

"Is that a water pump?" Amanda pointed to a big

lever by the sink. "Sweet." She raced over and put all her weight on the handle, trying to get it to move. "It's rusted shut."

Jasper, Clive, and Mitch showed off their muscles as they heaved, pushed, and pulled the handle. With a splat and a gurgle, thick, slimy sludge oozed out of the pipe and then water, the color of mud, dribbled out. As they kept pumping, the water became clearer. Soon we had a full bucket, a mop, rags we'd torn from the dusty bedclothes, and a broom. It felt good to work – it got my mind off our troubles as I sneezed my way through huge clouds of dust.

"Uh, everyone's pitching in," I pointed out to Sookie, who had pulled an ancient plaid shirt off a peg and was trying it on for size.

"This place doesn't look so bad to me." Sookie shrugged her shoulders.

"You've got to be kidding," said Mia, handing my sister a bucket and a mop. Sookie rolled up the sleeves of the enormous shirt.

Later I heard, "No, you have to dump the bucket and fill it with clean water again!" Sookie bossed Skeeter. "Otherwise you're mopping the floor with dirty water."

"I quit." Skeeter dropped the mop on the floor.

"Then I quit." Sookie turned in a huff and proceeded to advise Amarjeet on how to wash dishes.

Sookie was never much for tidying up – but she loved being a supervisor.

"How about both you and Skeeter dry the dishes," I said before she could drive Amarjeet crazy.

"Yeah," agreed Amarjeet. "Mop for five more

minutes, then both of you can come back and dry them."

After we'd cleaned up, we explored the cupboards, looking for anything we could possibly eat. "How long does tinned food last?" I asked.

Mia shrugged her shoulders. Then she said, "My mom makes me throw out any cans that are rusty or dented. That covers every can you've found."

With great reluctance, I tossed the cans. Their labels looked old-fashioned, so they were probably way past their expiration date anyway. Mitch had found matches and an oil lamp, which he lit and set on the table.

"Cat, do we *have* to dry the dishes?" asked Sookie "The tea towel is dirty." To demonstrate, Skeeter swiped a bowl and left muddy tracks.

"Never mind," said Clive, taking away the tea towel.

Mitch lit the stove with chopped kindling. That wood had been sitting by the stove and was pretty dry, so it burst into flame quickly. Amanda and Mia filled a pot with water and set it on the stove to boil. Mitch threw in plants and a freeze-dried package of the meat we'd salvaged from the bus's emergency kit. They took turns stirring the pot while the rest of us waited with watering mouths for the soup to bubble.

"Hey look, I found a bag of flour," I said with enthusiasm as I dug out the last object in the cupboard. "Maybe we can make some kind of biscuits to go with the soup." I imagined chomping into one and my stomach rumbled in anticipation.

"My grandmother used to make a type of bread called bannock just by using flour and water," said

Amanda.

"Why is the flour all speckled?" asked Sookie, who'd spilled some flour on the counter.

"Gross," said Skeeter, and I watched in horror as some of those specks began wiggling around. The menu ended up including only soup – we filled three pots and I downed so many bowls I swear my stomach sloshed.

The cabin grew warm and toasty. Whoever lived here had left it well stocked with wood. With a full stomach, and exhausted from the day, I grew drowsy.

Amarjeet rubbed her eyes. "Maybe there are mattresses or more blankets in the loft. We could use those to bed down."

"I'll check," Jasper said. He began climbing the stairs.

"Don't!" shouted Sookie. "Don't go up there, Jasper." She ran and grabbed his arm.

"Why not?" Jasper asked.

Sookie's face grew panicked and her eyes kept darting up to the loft. The rest of us crowded around the bottom of the steps.

"What's wrong?" I frowned.

"There's something up there," Sookie said in a hollow voice. "... something bad."

CHAPTER 17

The Nightmare Begins

WE STOOD AT the bottom of the rickety steps, staring up at the loft. Gloom lurked in the air, shrinking the cabin, and it felt as if a huge moth had fluttered its wings inside my stomach. I gulped. Sookie hadn't wanted to enter the cabin in the first place. Even though I didn't want to leave this comfortable shelter, which seemed a lot safer than the cold, wolf-ridden outdoors, I said quietly, "Should we get out of here?"

Sookie shook her head, "No." My sister scrunched her face trying to think of a way to explain herself. "It's just a feeling."

Clive leaned over and whispered into my ear. "Is this feeling her so-called magic?" Then, loud enough for Sookie to hear, he finished with, "Your mirror magic didn't work. We never found the creek."

Sookie regarded Clive in an unsettling way that made that moth in my stomach flap its wings again.

"I just asked the mirror which way we should turn," Sookie said simply. "I never asked for it to take us to the creek."

What did that mean? Clive snorted in disgust and charged up the steps. Jasper glanced at Sookie, clearly wanting to heed her warning. But with a half-apologetic nod, he followed Clive.

Maybe it wasn't the best idea, but I wanted to sleep *knowing* what was upstairs. Sookie didn't seem to want to go outside in the dark and cold any more than we did. But ...

"If there's something wrong up there, maybe it's best we know what it is," I decided. "Let's be careful."

It was pitch dark at the top of the stairs, but we stood outside the door until, slowly, Clive reached out to turn the door handle.

"Wait," I said. "We need more light."

"Could someone bring up the lamp?" Jasper called down.

Amarjeet rushed to get it while everyone else climbed the steps. Sookie began chanting.

"Here comes a candle to light you to bed. Here comes a chopper to chop off your head."

"Cut that out," Amanda snapped. "Is it always this spooky when you two are around?" Amanda regarded my sister and me with a curious stare. "Somehow I think so ..." Then she shook her head as if trying to wake from a bad dream.

I knew that feeling, but Amanda could shake her head all she wanted. She'd still be awake.

With a hand that only shook slightly, Amarjeet brought us the lamp and held it beside the door. Clive turned the handle, but just as the front door didn't budge at first, this door didn't either. Like before, the problem wasn't the lock, since the knob spun easily.

Once more, Clive, Mitch, and Jasper used their shoulders to slam against the door. Mia, Amarjeet, and I began kicking, while Amanda hovered at the top of the steps. We kept kicking and shoving, but this door was even harder to budge than the one downstairs.

"I'd listen to Sookie." Skeeter shook his head doubtfully. He stayed with Sookie on the lower step. It wasn't like Skeeter to skip out on any adventure. Come to think of it, Sookie was usually not this nervous either, except for that time when she'd had her first brush with ... *Fairy*.

The hair on the back of my neck bristled. I backed away, thinking it might be better to just leave the room alone. But I was too late. The door finally budged open. A strange smell poured out of the room, musty and dry as dust in an ancient crypt. I gagged slightly before sneezing.

Jasper and Clive began coughing, and then everybody began choking and sputtering. Something inside the room was barricading the door, and we couldn't open it completely. Between fits of coughing, the guys shoved and pushed until the door eased open. Clive stuck his head inside. Curiosity got the best of me – besides, the door was already open. I ducked under his shoulder to peer inside. Then I signaled Amarjeet to pass me the lamp.

"What is it? Is it a ghost?" Skeeter called to us.

I held the lamp just outside the door and strained to make out what was inside the dark murk.

Clive jabbed me in the ribs with his elbow and pointed to the floor inside the room. "Get a look at that," he said roughly, as if fighting the urge to shout.

A frayed, moth-eaten blanket lay on the cabin floor, bunched up in an odd shape, as if it was covering up a pile of kindling. Except ... it *wasn't* kindling.

A skeleton's arm poked out from under the blanket, its bony fingers stretching toward the window. Whoever the skeleton used to be had been trying to peer out the window ... *except the skeleton had no head.*

Jasper pushed me aside so he could take a better look. He inhaled sharply, catching his breath and holding it when he saw the headless skeleton. The others began crowding us, pushing us deeper into the room.

"What is it?" asked Amarjeet.

"Is something in there?" asked Mia.

"Whoa," said Mitch, as he stepped inside the door to check it out. "Don't ask."

But of course Mia and Amarjeet had to see it for themselves. They hissed in surprise when they saw the skeleton.

I was no longer looking at the floor. My attention was drawn to the huge window. Framed by ragged curtains, the window faced the back of the cabin. Outside, moonlight tumbled down into a small clearing and illuminated white stones laid out in a circle as big as my backyard.

And then, with no warning whatsoever, the window pane exploded. Glass flew everywhere. We jumped. Wind erupted inside the room, making the curtains flap and dance a garish, nasty jig like creepy shadow puppets. Silhouettes moved along the walls like unleashed phantoms.

"Back away!" I shouted to my friends. The wind inside the room whipped around the loft and grew in force. Air blasted my face, making my skin feel as if it were being pulled off like a Halloween mask. Dust whirled into the air, and as the air spun faster, yellowed papers, candlesticks, even a large bowl were sucked into the mini cyclone. We pulled ourselves out of the room and out of the wind. As I ran out, I looked back.

The growing tornado had gobbled up the curtains, the moth-eaten blanket, and the corpse's bones. I felt my feet lift from the ground and I grabbed the stair railing.

A wild, panicked thought struck me. *The wind will pull off my head.*

Then the door slammed shut.

"Let's get downstairs!" I shouted in a shaky voice. My legs were so wobbly I almost tumbled down the steps. Clive grabbed my arm and steadied me, but I shook my arm free so I could grasp the rail tighter.

Carefully, we all made our way downstairs. I couldn't rid myself of the notion that opening the door had somehow altered the cabin. I could no longer trust the walls and floor to stay solid. But I couldn't think of a good reason why. I heard the wind in the loft die with one last gasp, as suddenly as it had risen.

For a panicked second, I couldn't spot Sookie. I lifted the lamp and swung it around the room. Finally I could make out her shape against the far wall, joined by Amanda and Skeeter. They had pulled apart the cobweb curtains and were staring out the window at the back of the cabin. We joined them.

Sookie turned to me and said, "Now you've done it, Cat. You've opened the door."

"No, we closed it," I said. Well, the rushing wind had closed it.

"I don't think that's the door she means," said Amanda in a haunted voice as she stared out the window.

CHAPTER 18

Night Terrors

I JOINED THE others at the window. Skeeter, Sookie, and Amanda were looking at the strange pile of stones outside. The stones were arranged in a circle and in spokes, like a wheel. In the moonlight the stones looked eerie – almost as if they were gaping skulls.

Amanda pointed to the stone circle and said in a peculiar, strangled voice, "This cabin is built on top of a doorway to the Otherworld." Then she turned and stared at me. "Remember how you were asking about a place of power, Cat? Well, you're looking at a place of power."

The way Amanda was pointing out the window reminded me of the grisly sight I'd just seen in the loft, of the skeleton jabbing its bony hand in the same direction, except that Amanda still had her head.

"I ... I ... know what those stones are," Amanda continued nervously. "It's a medicine wheel and a medicine wheel is built upon a place of power ... sometimes great power."

"That's what you wanted, wasn't it?" Clive glanced doubtfully at Sookie. "... to find a place of power."

"Yeah," said Mitch. "Now you can use that mirror of yours and get us out of here."

Amarjeet shook her head. "Somehow I don't think it's

going to be that easy."

"Well," I asked my sister. "Is this what you were talking about? Can those stones help you work the mirror magic?"

Sookie's eyes grew so wide they threatened to swallow the only bit of light in the room. Her small face paled. She shook her head slowly as if she was confused. "Cat, this place scares me. Maybe there's too much power."

The hair on the back of my neck had been rising ever since we'd discovered this place – or it discovered us. Sookie had almost been pulled deep into dark magic this spring – and now she was trying to tell me that she felt that sinister tug again!

I tried to shake my uneasiness. The problem was the tables had been turned. This time we *needed* magic to get us out of trouble. Even though this place was spooky and we'd just had a fright, we were lost and exhausted. We had to get home from Headless Valley in one piece. That might be impossible without a little magical help.

I tried joking around to settle Sookie's nerves. "Place of great power, huh? I don't see any posh school nearby. There are no posters here to join a soccer match." But the joke died on my lips because only Jasper's eyes flashed with any recognition of that time in the past – and he wasn't smiling. Since last Halloween, when we discovered a fairy school had sat on top of Grim Hill, spewing its evil magic like an active volcano, our lives had never been the same. But everyone else in town had fallen under its enchantment and couldn't remember what had happened. Just thinking about the past made my feather, which was supposed to help me remember, sear with a heat that burned through my jeans, almost scorching my skin. There was magic around here – plenty of it.

"I ... I ... guess I can try and use the fairy mirror," Sookie said. But then she pulled her gaze away from the window, came over, and grabbed my hand. In her quiet, little girl voice she whispered, "I don't want to be a witch, Cat. Not really." I tightened my hand over hers protectively.

"So far you've only used your magic to help us – that's not *maleficium*." If you used magic against someone bad – that wasn't dark magic, was it? "No, of course you don't have to be a witch." We were in total agreement there. Also I was heartened that the little magic my sister had used hadn't brought her closer to the edge. There hadn't been any bad consequences. Still ...

"Maybe we don't even need the mirror," I said. "If we just find our way back to the road, then we can use the bus radio to call for help."

"Now you're talking sense," Clive said. But he didn't look so cocky this time.

Amanda yanked the cobweb curtains over the window and I felt strangely relieved – almost as if the medicine wheel had been staring at us and not vice versa. The gloom in the place seemed to lift and the dark felt less oppressive.

"Let's get some sleep," suggested Amarjeet.

"Girls can have the space closest to the stove," Clive offered. "We men, I mean, guys, can camp out closer to the door."

The night had plunged into a chilling freeze and we fanned out from the stove. Too much of an icy draft radiated from the old door so we coaxed the guys closer. Mitch stacked the stove with a heavy log which would burn slowly through the night.

Sookie and I stretched out beside each other. We used my backpack for a pillow and my sister snuggled up against me. There were no spruce boughs beneath us like in the shelter and the floor was cold and hard. It was uncomfortable and I figured I'd never fall asleep. That lasted about two seconds.

* * *

I awoke in the deepest, darkest part of the night. A horrible stench of rotting dead things and moldering old fur clogged my nose and left a disgusting taste in my mouth.

Slump, thump, creak. Something was after us, something awful. It had climbed through the loft window and was moving downstairs in lumbering, deadly steps, lurching toward us. For a moment I thought I was dreaming –

"Did you hear that?" Mia whispered harshly in the dark. Okay, so it wasn't a dream.

"Somebody's upstairs," said another voice – Jasper's.

There was a rustling sound and then a few groggy voices. "Huh?"

I shot up to a sitting position, but it was too dark to see anything. The oil lamp Amarjeet had set on the table had burned out. There was only a tiny red glow from behind the stove door.

"Clive." I stretched out my leg and shoved his

shoulder with my foot. "Wake up."

"Nhug?" was Clive's mumbled response, then, "Huh?" Like me, he shot straight up and sprang into action.

We heard a deep, rumbling growl that sent chills over every square inch of me and set my heart racing. Mitch, who was closest to the stairs, jumped up with a yelp. A huge, black shadow moved like a wraith between the railing slats at the top of the loft.

"Grab pots and pans and whatever you can use to make noise," I shouted.

"And we need weapons – use sticks, the mop, broom, anything," yelled Clive.

We stumbled around in the dark cabin, grabbing whatever we could get our hands on, and charged toward the stairs.

We crowded around the bottom step, yelling, shouting, and making as much noise as we could. At the top of the stairs stood the black shadow, a hulking silhouette that growled and snapped in a menacing sneer. It hesitated, but I swear I didn't know if I'd be able to stand my ground if it lunged forward. Except I had no choice – we were in this together and I had to protect Sookie.

Suddenly a vivid flash of light illuminated the cabin in a ghostly green glow. The gigantic black creature snarled at us, revealing dripping fangs the length of my finger. Its eyes glowed a menacing yellow. This was no wolf I'd ever read about. A rolling thunderclap made the walls inside the cabin shudder and I heard more glass break upstairs. The black monster slinked back up the top steps. With a sinister growl, it disappeared into the room and the door slammed shut behind it.

This time I made sure of it. I moved so fast, I didn't have time to think about the consequences. I flew up the stairs and threw my weight into the door, but it really was closed. I turned to flee but ran straight into Clive and Jasper.

"Jam it with this," Clive said, handing me a broomstick. I wedged it under the door handle.

"And use this," said Jasper, jamming a kitchen knife into the doorframe.

As soon as Jasper placed the knife, I heard more glass smash inside the room and then an eerie silence.

CHAPTER 19

A Menacing Fiend

"WHAT *WAS* THAT?" Blood pounded in my ears. Once more I checked the broomstick jammed under the door handle. It seemed firm.

We returned to the others and Amarjeet filled the lamp again. The feeble glow of the wick barely lit the dusty glass bowl.

"That was some wolf." Skeeter whistled appreciatively.

"That was no wolf," I said. Or at least not one I'd ever read about in my research.

"One of those legends my grandmother used to tell me about, only now I don't think they were legends at all," Amanda said softly, "was about a creature called the *waheela,* a bear-wolf that haunts the forests surrounding Headless Valley." Amanda's eyes grew round with fear. "Again, I thought that was just another stupid kid's story to keep us from wandering in the woods. But she's been right about so many things." Her eyes blinked rapidly. "If only I'd paid more attention to her."

"Those creatures looked familiar to me as well," Jasper said slowly. He raised his hands to his eyes, remembered he no longer wore glasses, and then just rubbed his face. That meant he was deep in thought. He found his pack and yanked out one of his pocketbooks.

Come to think of it, he'd never torn up a single book, even when we were looking for paper to build a fire.

Jasper brought his book to the table and laid it beneath the oil lamp. He adjusted the knob on the lamp to increase the flame, and in the brighter glow, flipped through the pages. I leaned over his shoulder – he was reading a book on Celtic legends. Since our fairy trouble Jasper was always researching the Celts. Jasper signaled me to move because my shadow was darkening the pages. I stepped back, hugging my arms and glancing up at the loft as we all hovered around the lamp in heavy silence.

"Ah," Jasper said, but not in a good way.

"What?" I practically dived back to the table.

"Remember when we were running to the cabin," Jasper explained. "We ran through a bog."

I nodded, and even as he said that I recalled the overpowering stench I'd woken up to. It was as if the dank smell of the bog had followed us here.

"Well," said Jasper. "The Celts believed evil creatures inhabited bogs. They called them fiends."

"We're not exactly in Ireland," said Clive.

"That doesn't matter," explained Jasper. "When we were in Sweden, they practiced Walpurgis, which was a Celtic festival."

"Something happened on Walpurgis Night when we were in Sweden, didn't it, Cat?" Amarjeet fastened her no-nonsense stare on me. "I keep having a weird dream about it."

Mia nodded in agreement, her chin bobbing almost

frantically. Clive's expression became thoughtful and I wondered if he was remembering how we'd been captured. *That's right,* whispered a voice inside me. *You've been in tight spots before and worked them out, Cat. Take hope.*

"Once more," Clive struggled to stay patient. He didn't snap at any of us, so I had to give him credit for that. "What does Sweden or Celts have to do with that ... um, creature we chased away."

Jasper held his book in front of our noses. On the page was an illustration of a huge, black, diabolical beast with hunched shoulders, gaping jaws, and blood red eyes. Except for the eyes, it was very similar to the creature we'd just seen.

"That's a *waheela,*" Amanda assured us. "My grandmother drew me a picture of one once. She told me the *waheela* was like a giant wolf with supernatural powers and ... and ..."

"Tell us," demanded Clive. "We need to know."

Amanda swallowed. "She used to say this forest was infested with evil spirits, and that the *waheela* was responsible for the headless corpses."

For a while nobody said anything. Then Jasper broke the silence. "Your grandmother's bear-wolf and the Celts' fiend are probably the same thing – a creature from the Otherworld."

Amanda nodded. "Grandmother told me to always remember that we walk in two worlds at the same time, ours and the Otherworld."

"Your grandmother is wise," said Jasper gently.

Almost in a whisper, Amanda replied, "I know

that now."

"Fiend, *waheela*, who cares?" said Clive. "The question is: how did it get upstairs?"

Then Sookie said a funny thing. "Because you opened the door."

"No," I explained to both Sookie and Clive. "The creature crawled in through the broken window. We'd left the door shut – the wind must have blown it open again."

"That makes sense," said Clive.

But Sookie only shook her head and didn't say anything more.

Mitch and Clive had found a hammer and nails in a kitchen drawer. They pulled apart the dilapidated table and hammered its boards across the loft door. Amarjeet, Mia, and I threaded pots and pans with old string we'd found in another kitchen drawer. We then strung the clattering line across the top of the stairs to sound an alarm. It wouldn't scare off a *waheela*, but it would give us more warning.

It occurred to me that the creature had behaved a little like a wolf. Wolves learned by stalking and watching new prey. They were clever and could even unlatch gates ... or, I gulped, doors. Then, as if to mock me, chilling howls ripped through the night.

The fiend wasn't far away and it had friends. Those creatures had been stalking us and the one we had seen today must be the scout. They were getting braver – that was *not* good.

All of us huddled in a circle around the stove. Skeeter was keeping the fire going with his usual gusto. Clive had to grab the wood out of his brother's hand when the flames roared and the stove grew red hot. My forehead broke into a sweat.

We had to try and rest for the remaining hours of the night, since we'd had almost no sleep the last three nights. I nearly laughed when I remembered that I wasn't able to sleep two nights ago because I'd be visiting my new high school the next day. Good one, Cat – new teachers and older students didn't seem so scary anymore.

We lay down, but it wasn't easy for anyone to drift back to sleep. Amarjeet snapped at Jasper, accusing him of kicking her. Mitch and Mia bickered about whose idea it had been to hike back to the bus. Skeeter snarled at Clive when his older brother took the wood away and forbade him to put any more in the stove. I thought I heard Amanda sniffle, but she'd rolled onto her stomach and her arm covered her face. Once more I cozied up to Sookie.

* * *

A flash of green light on my face made my eyes flutter open. Clive was snoring softly and Jasper sighed in his sleep. The lamp had once again gone out and the cabin was cloaked in murky darkness. So where was that light coming from? That was when I noticed Sookie was missing.

A bright beam flashed across the room. Was it lightning? I spotted Sookie. She was standing by the window. She'd pulled the cobweb curtains away from the glass, revealing the stone medicine circle outside. Harsh moonlight beamed through. But that wasn't what was making light flash across the room.

My sister was humming an unearthly tune under the lunar light. She held a silver object in her left hand – Lea's fairy mirror. Moonlight reflected back from the mirror, painting my sister's face with ghostly illumination. I swear she no longer looked like a child of this world.

Then my heart stopped.

The mirror flashed once more and I heard someone singing back.

CHAPTER 20

Disturbing Visions

"SOOKIE," I RASPED. "What are you doing?" This didn't make sense. A short time ago my sister had told me she wanted to stay away from magic. So why was she playing with the mirror now?

Did she say that, Cat? that annoying voice in my head piped up. *She said she didn't want to be a witch, but she didn't mention staying away from magic.* A cold lump of ice formed inside my stomach and I remembered how my plans always backfired. But not this time, I swore to myself. My sister wasn't going to become a witch. We were going to avoid that trap – that terrible fate that ran in our family – one sister becoming a fairy fighter, the other turning into a witch.

"Put away the fairy mirror, Sookie," I urged her.

"It's okay, Cat." Sookie's voice sounded faint, as if it had to travel a great distance. "I'm sure now I can use the mirror to call for help."

"What do you mean?" I took a step closer, reaching for Lea's mirror, but Sookie snatched her hand away.

"Hey," I said in a warning tone, putting my hands on my hips.

"I can reach people through this mirror, Cat."

"Which people?" I asked suspiciously. Then I shook

my head. "Forget it. I think you'd better hand it over." I held out my hand, determined to take back my mirror.

"People you want to see," Sookie said.

My hand stopped in mid-air. "Who?" Then I repeated more forcefully, "Exactly what are you seeing in that mirror?"

"I can see a lot of things," Sookie said coyly. "Come look for yourself."

I stepped closer to Sookie, letting the cold moonlight wash over me. Then I leaned over my sister's shoulder and stared into the fairy mirror. At first it was foggy, just as the glass had always appeared since I got it. Then slowly the fog lifted. I could see shapes forming in the looking glass. "No," I gasped.

I was staring into my own living room, where I could see Mom. My eyes began stinging and I blinked back the tears. She was sitting on our couch with a quilt tugged over her shoulders. She had fallen asleep sitting up. The telephone was on her lap, and her fingers stayed close to the receiver. Crumpled paper cups, half-filled with coffee, littered the coffee table. Stacked plates carried sandwiches that had only one or two bites nibbled out of them. Balled up Kleenex tumbled from her lap into a huge pile on the rug.

Shadows circled Mom's eyes and her hair stuck out in every direction. Her blouse wasn't tucked in to her skirt and it looked like she'd slept in her work clothes more than once. I didn't know my heart could ache so much. "We've got to get back to Mom fast, Sookie."

My sister nodded. The mirror swirled with mist again and when it cleared I felt a shock run through me. Staring right back at us through the looking glass was Great Aunt Hildegaard. She regarded us with a stern expression, waved her finger at Sookie, and shook her head. Then she spotted me hovering above my sister, or at least that's how it seemed. My aunt wasn't pleased with us. Worse, a deep sadness fell over her face.

Sookie shook the mirror and mist fogged up the glass again. "That's enough for now," she said bossily.

She had that right. After a short tussle, I won back the mirror from my sister.

"I didn't do anything wrong," Sookie complained. "The mirror summoned me."

"What?" That so didn't sound good.

As if reading my mind, my kid sister said, "It's okay, Cat. It was Lea. She knew we were in trouble and she's sending us help."

My jaw dropped and I gaped at her. I never thought I'd see my friend again. "Get her back," I said quickly.

"Then hand me the mirror," Sookie ordered.

I almost did. That's how badly I wanted to see my friend once more. Maybe it was the greedy expression on my sister's face. Maybe it was those moth wings brushing against my stomach again. But suddenly I was overwhelmed with the notion that giving my sister back the mirror was the worst thing I could do. I turned and went back to where we'd slept. "No," I said, stuffing the mirror back into my pack. I slipped my backpack over my shoulder. Let her try and sneak the mirror out now.

"Do you two never sleep ... wait, what's that smell? Is that smoke?" Mia sniffed and coughed. "Wake up everyone!"

she shouted. "The cabin is filling up with smoke."

I'd been so transfixed by the mirror, I hadn't even noticed the smoke. There was no mistaking it now – thick black clouds curled out from inside the stove. My throat began to burn and water streamed from my eyes.

Suddenly the stove exploded into searing flames that ate through the wall farthest from us. Everyone screamed and scrambled for the front door. "Sookie!" I ran to get my sister. Another explosion echoed in my ears, muffling all other noise. It was like I was stuck in slow motion and no matter how fast I moved, I couldn't cover enough ground. Finally, I made it across the room. I could barely make out my sister's blond head in the stinging black smoke. I grabbed her hand.

But when I turned to flee, I saw a line of yellow flames dancing between us and the cabin door.

CHAPTER 21

A Dark Despair

FLAMES QUICKLY ENGULFED the cabin, trapping Sookie and me inside. I felt as if I'd been sunburned and I coughed as hot air seared my lungs. "Sookie, cover yourself with this," I rasped.

My eyes streamed with tears in the thick, black smoke while I yanked off my pack and unzipped my windbreaker. I bundled Sookie in my jacket, making sure it covered her face. The dry, dust-tattered curtains had burst into flames and hot ashes drifted down, biting into my skin. I slammed my backpack through the window, breaking the glass. Burning air rushed toward us and long flames stretched like arms.

I was about to kick out the rest of the glass when the window exploded, its dagger-like shards narrowly missing Sookie and me. But the broken glass had cleared enough room for us to escape. I grabbed my sister and jumped out, landing on top of Clive.

"Ugh," he said as I knocked the wind out of him.

"We were pulling away the broken glass to get you out," said Jasper.

I jumped up and brushed shards of glass off my jeans. "Is everyone else okay?"

Jasper wiped a smear of soot off his face. With a

cough, he said, "Yes."

"Sookie, are you all right?" She nodded.

"Uh, you're welcome," Clive said, taking a deep breath and standing up.

"Thanks, Clive," I said. "It was a very soft landing."

"Let's get out of here," said Jasper.

The cabin was burning up like a torch and a series of explosions sent parts of the roof flying. Smoking shingles littered the ground. One narrowly missed my head as it flew by.

"Run!" shouted Mitch.

It wasn't until we were away from the cabin that I looked around to see where we had stopped. Great. We were standing in the center of the medicine circle – the place of power. In the dawn light it had lost some of its eerie glow, but I felt as if I were standing below a transmission tower. A steady high-pitched whine buzzed in my ears, accompanying the haunting rhythm of the relentless wind.

"Did either of you get burned?" asked Mia. Then her face crumpled. "Oh no, the first aid kit got left behind." Her face fell even more. "Everything got left behind."

"I'm fine," I said, breaking into a fit of coughing. "Sookie?"

My sister rubbed her eyes, which gave her soot-streaked face the appearance of a raccoon. In a shaky voice, she answered. "Yes, Cat, I'm okay."

It was then I noticed that she was clutching my backpack to her chest. Was that all we had left – my pack and that stupid mirror? "Did anybody get *anything* out of the cabin?"

Everyone shook their head. "When you were trapped, we ran around to the other side of the cabin to get you out," said Clive. "There wasn't time to get our stuff."

I nodded. So that was it: we were stranded in the far north, we were lost, and we had no food, water, or blankets. Not to mention we were already half-starved.

Pink light streaked the sky as the sun began to rise. The air was frigid, and despite the searing heat of the cabin, we all began to shiver.

"I'm cold and I'm hungry. Clive," said Skeeter, "can we build another shelter?"

"Good idea," said Clive.

Then Skeeter rubbed his stomach. "We need to find some breakfast first."

Clive patted his brother's shoulder. "I don't think we'll find a pancake place around here," he said quietly

"Berries don't cut it," Skeeter grumbled. "All I can think about is real food." Then he gave up and sat down in the dirt. No one had the energy to move let alone cheer each other on. Our despair was contagious.

But the most dangerous thing I could do was sit down and give up. "Come on," I said. "The explosions have stopped. We can all move closer to the cabin and at least stay warm."

Even though we never said anything to each other, it was easy to tell nobody liked staying inside the stone circle. Despite our exhaustion, we returned to the front of the cabin. Most of the flames had died down, leaving only a pile of smoldering wood and ash.

The warmth cheered us up a little. "I think those are salmonberry bushes over there. We can gather some for breakfast," Amanda said eventually. She nudged Skeeter. "Come on, it will be better than nothing."

"If you can find any of those roots we had before, I'll cook them on the hot ashes," Mitch said.

"But I'm so thirsty." Skeeter's voice quavered.

"The berries will help your thirst," Amanda replied. Slowly we all got moving, and doing something felt better than doing nothing at all. Still, nobody mentioned hiking out of here. Nobody mentioned anything about what we should do next. Including me. I just didn't know what we could do – should we wait to be rescued or strike out and hope for the best?

I wiped salmonberry juice from my mouth. It had soothed my aching throat, but I swear I would need to devour all the leaves on the bush before I would feel full. Every muscle in my body ached and my skin stung. If only I could get my brain to work, but it was as if a fog had taken hold of it. No clear thoughts were coming through. A sense of urgency rose inside me. We needed a plan – and we needed it soon.

"We should try hiking back to the road, maybe?" suggested Mia. "This place gives me the creeps."

"And if we don't find the bus? What if we end up even deeper inside this forest?" Anxiety edged into Clive's voice.

"Everyone thought it was a good idea yesterday," Mia protested.

I wanted to get out of here myself. Except ... "What if someone spotted the flames from the cabin? They'd come and check, wouldn't they?"

"There was a thunderstorm last night, remember?" Clive argued. "They'd assume lightning hit a tree."

"Make up your mind, Clive. Do you want to stay or go," Mia said petulantly.

"It's not that easy," Clive grumbled.

"It's also pointless now," Jasper said.

"What do you mean?" His tone unnerved me.

Jasper pointed over my shoulder. "We've got company."

I turned and followed his gaze. The bus driver, the pilot, and the thug strode out of the bushes. Each of them was carrying a gun, which they pointed at us, and each of their faces broke into identical evil grins.

CHAPTER 22

Sookie's Mistake

THE MEN HERDED us into a tight group. They pointed their guns straight at us – except when Sookie broke into a sob, the driver lowered his gun and stared at her apologetically. That's when I had my brilliant idea.

I caught Jasper's attention and pointed to the ground. Shards of window glass were at our feet. "Ah," I groaned. "Those berries hurt my stomach." I doubled over and screamed. At least that's what the criminals saw and heard. Meanwhile, Jasper had scooped up two pieces of glass.

"Shut up," ordered the pilot.

For good measure, I groaned and screamed again.

"I said shut up." The pilot strode toward me and for a panicked second I thought he was going to hit me with the butt of his rifle. It was one thing to see violence on TV, another to actually face it. My stomach really did cramp up while my heart pounded in my chest.

"Don't you touch her." Clive grabbed the pilot's arm, which was probably an insane thing to do. For a heart-stopping moment I thought he might shoot Clive, but instead the pilot shoved him to the ground.

"Where are the diamonds?" he asked as he yanked Clive back off the ground.

"Leave my brother alone or I'll ..." Skeeter raised his fists, but Amarjeet quickly swept Skeeter into her arms, holding him back.

"I'm done with chasing you kids around," spat the pilot. "I'm going to ask you one last time – where are the diamonds?"

The brutish thug hovered over Mia and glared at us with menace, while the pilot jammed a gun into Clive's chest. The driver held his gun just above our heads, but his arm shook badly.

"The diamonds were inside," I said, pointing to the cabin.

"There was a fire," said Jasper, stating the obvious. "We didn't get them out in time."

"What?" roared the pilot. "Tie these brats up," he ordered the other two. "I don't need them wandering away while we wait for the ashes to cool."

The driver and the thug pulled out a long stretch of rope from their pack. They made us sit back to back in a circle and wove the rope in and out, tying our hands behind us.

My plan couldn't have worked out better.

* * *

While the men huddled us together, Jasper slipped a piece of glass to me. I shoved part of the glass into my back pocket, enough so that it wouldn't jab me, and so that I could grasp the part that was poking out even though my hands were tied. I just hadn't counted on being so nervous that my hands would sweat. I hoped Clive didn't mind me drying my damp palms on the back of his shirt.

As soon as the ashes had cooled enough for the men to sift through them, Jasper and I got to work. With a slow, deep breath, I slid the glass shard out of my pocket and angled it so I could saw through the rope. I felt the rope fray and within a few seconds, strands began to break. But I couldn't slice too far into the rope or I'd slash my own skin. Better to keep pulling at the rope and feel the give. Soon I was able to tug my hands free and I immediately set to work sawing through Clive's knot. I passed the glass to Clive and he began freeing Mia, while Jasper handed his shard of glass to Amarjeet. Soon we were all untied.

Now all we had to do was sneak into the forest while the outlaws sifted through the ashes. We quietly crept into the bushes, first Skeeter and Sookie, then Mia and Mitch. Sweat beaded on my forehead even though we were sitting away from the smoldering cabin, while wind sliced through the chilly air. But we didn't dare leave together – the noise might alert the criminals.

Finally, Amarjeet and I crawled into the brush, with Jasper and Clive directly behind us. We'd made it. I stretched and let out another slow, silent breath. We had to get moving – as to where, I had no idea.

"My mirror," Sookie cried out. "I forgot the backpack."

Before I could grab her, Sookie ran to where we'd been tied up. I took off after her but Amarjeet grabbed my arm, signaling with her finger for me to stay super quiet. I moved toward my sister and watched with slow horror as she brushed off a pile of rope and picked up my backpack.

Sookie turned, ready to join us. But by then it was too late.

"Come out at once or the girl's dead."

The pilot turned away from the ashes and pointed his gun at my sister.

CHAPTER 23

A Grave Plan

I COULDN'T BELIEVE that the pilot, however horrid he was, would actually shoot a kid. The problem was I couldn't disbelieve it either – not after what we'd heard on the two-way radio. My friends felt the same way and we all filed out of the bushes. The outlaws herded us back into the clearing. We'd almost gotten away, but because of my little sister we were captured again. Why hadn't she just left the stupid pack behind?

Sookie must have seen the outrage on my face because she mumbled, "I'm sorry, Cat."

"It's not just me," I whispered harshly. "You've put everyone in jeopardy." Sookie hung her head.

"Just what's so important about this pack, little missy," said the pilot, grabbing it from my sister's hands.

I flinched when he said that. Mom called Sookie "missy" when she lectured her. Coming from *him*, that word sounded foul.

The pilot unzipped the pack and said, "Maybe there's something very important in here. The diamonds, perhaps?"

The outlaw began yanking out the cowboy pajamas I'd packed. Mom had bought them for me on sale, as a joke – it had been a fun idea for a sleepover, but it wasn't so funny right now. It seemed years since I'd planned to have a sleepover at Mia's. Then he yanked Lea's mirror out of the bag. The mirror sparkled in the sun and gave off its usual greenish light. The pilot didn't seem to notice. He threw it down and Sookie cried out when the mirror cracked.

Then my sister said in that strange hollow voice she sometimes used, "You've done it now, breaking that mirror. Your luck will be cursed."

It wasn't so much what she said, but the effect it had. Her words raised the hair on the back of *my* neck. Even the pilot paused for a second and stared at my sister.

"You brats had too much time on your hands before," he said angrily. "No more sitting around making trouble."

He pointed his rifle at us and gestured that we move toward the smoldering ashes. There wasn't much else left of the cabin. "*You* search for the diamonds. I'm taking a break."

Rubbing his chin, he said, "Come to think of it, this is a much better idea. All of you can look through the ashes while me and my buddies stand guard."

His voice dropped into an even more menacing tone. "And you'd better find those diamonds fast."

We waded into the ashes. As we moved closer, I saw that, bizarrely enough, the loft door was still intact. The heat seared through my sneakers – we weren't wearing heavy hiking boots like the men. I hopped from foot to foot, then dug a burnt stick out of the ashes. I waved the stick around, cooling it, and then handed it to my sister. "Use this to dig around for the diamonds." Sookie took the stick and began to poke halfheartedly at the ashes.

It was slow, hot work. My back ached and the soles of my feet blistered. Part of me knew we had to draw this out as long as possible, so we'd have a better chance of being rescued. Another part of me wanted to give up, dig up the diamonds, and get it over with. *Don't even think it,* I said to myself.

"Aah!" screamed Amanda. The crooks jumped up and ran toward her. But she hadn't stumbled on diamonds – it was the charred rib of the headless skeleton. Her nerves just about had it when they forced her to dig through the rest of the ashes, which were mixed with pieces of bone. Tears streaked down her soot-smeared face.

Their cruelty made my blood boil. I edged my way through the sooty remains to help Amanda. When I passed Clive, he leaned forward and whispered, "We're in deep."

Like I didn't know. Then Clive went on to say, "As soon as somebody finds the diamonds, we're goners. We have to be super-alert and seize the first opportunity to escape again."

I had to hand it to Clive. Like any good team player, he never called it quits. As long as the game was in play, he'd give it his all. He played soccer that way as well and had even scored tying goals in the last three seconds of a game. A sharp pang rose inside me – I sure hoped I'd be able to play soccer again. *Don't go there, Cat,* that voice in my head advised me. *Focus on the moment.*

The pilot had made himself nice and comfortable. He sat on a log, slurping from a water bottle and munching on a power bar. As I watched him, my stomach grumbled and my throat ached. *He* definitely wasn't paying close attention. His muscle-bound accomplice had his gun pointed at us, but his head was turned toward the pilot. They were having a lively conversation about how rich they would soon become.

Only the bus driver was watching us closely. His quivering hands still shook his rifle as he kept guard over us, and his eyes darted nervously back and forth from the other two men to us. I'd already figured out he was their lackey, the lowest crook on the totem pole. Maybe at this moment he was wondering why his buddies weren't including him in the conversation about how to spend all the money. I realized he was the weakest link – and our best chance at getting out of here.

Maybe we couldn't wait for the first opportunity. Maybe we had to create one. Even though I thought my very soul might split apart, I knew what I had to do. No matter how I figured it, there was no other way out.

It's okay, Cat, I consoled myself. *Sookie won't be using her magic for evil – this will be for the good of us all ...*

Slowly, as nonchalantly as my pounding heart allowed, I paid all of the others a quick visit while pretending to search for the diamonds. It was time for us to act as a soccer team. In a whisper, I explained my plan to deke and dodge, and as I walked around, the tension among us became as thick as syrup.

I made my way toward the bus driver. I checked to make sure the other two men were still lost in conversation. They were. I whispered, "What if I could show you where the diamonds are first, before I tell those guys?"

The driver stared at me, and when he didn't say anything, I took that as encouragement. My throat felt like sandpaper when I swallowed. "What if, say, you had time to slip a couple of diamonds in your own pocket before we called out to them?" I tilted my head toward the other crooks.

The driver still said nothing, but he was looking at me intently. "All we ask for in return is when we run off, you shoot over our heads," I finished.

This time the driver gave the slightest nod.

CHAPTER 24

Mirror Madness

EVEN IF THE driver shot over our heads, I wasn't sure he'd miss with his hands shaking so much. Not that it mattered. We only wanted him to *think* we were going to escape. My goal was to buy us time to carry out my plan. Driving a wedge between the bus driver and his partners would also help at the critical moment.

"The little kids get to go first," I instructed the driver. "You have to let them slip out before we show you where the diamonds are. They need a head start."

The driver didn't move a muscle, but sweat beaded on his forehead. He wanted those diamonds and he didn't want to shoot us, but he was still afraid the other men would be on to him – could we trust him?

Taking a deep breath, I decided we had to take that chance. I edged over to Sookie. "I'm sorry, but I just can't see any other way. This will be our only chance ... are you sure it will work?"

Sookie nodded solemnly, her face calm and confident. "It will work, Cat."

I couldn't believe what I was about to do. But our time had run out. Even if the driver let all of us escape, and I doubted he would, we wouldn't get far. We were dead lost with no food or water, all of us starved and thirsty.

Our legs would not outrun determined, equipped criminals. Even if they left us alone, they'd be right in thinking we wouldn't survive another night.

My heart grew heavy as stone at what I was about to do and my stomach twisted into an uncomfortable knot. I'll admit it – even though everything about this felt wrong, I said the words anyways.

"Sookie, conjure the most powerful magic you can. Save us."

My sister nodded. "Remember, Cat. When I use the mirror to make the summons, everyone has to be inside the medicine circle. Or they will be in danger."

An icy dread swept through me. Sookie's magic always caused trouble, but as far as I could see, at this point trading trouble would give us more hope. Squaring my shoulders, I counted off my fingers for the signals. One, two, three – my team fell into place.

Amanda, Mia, and Mitch spread themselves strategically among the cabin ruins, in their soccer positions of goalie and left and right defense. They cut off the vantage point to the back of the cabin, which prevented the crooks from seeing Sookie and Skeeter make their way to the medicine wheel. My little sister snuck away clutching the backpack that held the mirror she guarded so carefully.

Next Amarjeet, Jasper, and Clive moved into left wing, center, and right wing positions, and they lined up, ready for action. That made me the soccer ball. I moved toward the spot where Clive had slept last night. He'd told me the diamonds would be about fourteen steps to the left of the burnt-out stove. While it looked as if the others were picking and searching, I was the one moving amongst the ashes, pushing them around with my stick until I spotted blackened lumps of rock. I made the last signal – then moved in the opposite direction and bent over as if to pick something up.

While the driver's eyes focused on me, I sensed – rather than heard – Sookie chanting in the distance. Strange. Even though she must've been whispering, I swear her voice blended with the howling wind, making her words sound cold and hard, like the diamonds. I hoped the pilot and thug couldn't hear her.

"Fo-the-oh-rum," she chanted. *"Fia-eh-s-gohe ..."*

Sweat broke out on my forehead and back, but the wind quickly dried it, leaving me chilled. As her words wove in and out in a peculiar dance, so did my friends. Mitch, Mia, and Amanda edged toward the medicine circle, and Clive, Jasper, and Amarjeet moved toward me.

While the driver watched, Amarjeet plucked the blackened diamonds from the ashes and made her way to the edge of the cabin, within sight of the other crooks. She dropped the stones there. Jasper and Clive moved in for the final move.

When I stood up, pretending to hold something in my hand, the driver leapt toward me. He hadn't planned to let us escape at all. Just as I figured – he couldn't face what would happen to Sookie and Skeeter, but he was too afraid of the other guys to let us all go. He only wanted to use us to find the diamonds first.

Jasper and Clive threw ashes in his face. He slumped onto his knees with a cry. The other crooks jumped up, but they didn't have time to unholster their rifles before Amarjeet scrambled toward the medicine circle.

"What's going on here?" shouted the pilot. Then he spotted the diamonds Amarjeet had collected, with the driver slumped over them. "Looks like you are making your own little stash," he grumbled at the driver.

The plan was working – as far as the crooks were concerned, diamonds first, kill the kids second. When they bent over to scoop up the diamonds, we stood there innocently, that is until Jasper and Clive threw ashes in their faces too. They stumbled around blindly – the pilot groaned and rubbed a hot cinder out of one eye.

Lightning cracked through the sky and immediately a clap of thunder made a horrendous explosion, shaking the ground. I turned back to run for the medicine wheel when I lost my balance and fell, landing face first into hot ashes. My skin burned, but luckily I'd shut my eyes. When I tried getting up, though, I couldn't move – someone had grabbed my legs. The driver!

"Hurry, Cat," Mia called. My skin blistered as I lifted my chin and struggled to break free. I hoped the rest of my friends had made it back in time.

The wind began howling in an unbearable wail, as dirt and ash and even pieces of lumber lifted and fell dangerously around us. The driver tugged me toward him. My shirt rode up and a hot stone burned against my stomach.

"Ugh," groaned the driver.

My legs were suddenly free and somebody hoisted me to my feet. Jasper had thrown more ashes into the driver's face and Clive had pulled me up. We raced toward our friends.

I held my hand over my face, shielding my eyes as the wind whipped around us. A burnt chair leg flew by, narrowly missing me, but a charred piece of shingle caught me sharply on my arm. I swear my feet were lifting off the ground even before I made it inside the peculiar calm of the medicine wheel.

We waited inside the circle as we watched the remains of the cabin sweep up into a swirling tornado. Mia screamed and we all dived to the side as the loft door flew up and over our heads, landing upright and embedding itself in the center of the medicine circle.

The outlaws ran from the destruction of the cabin and headed toward our circle. I pulled my eyes off them and checked on Sookie.

An eerie light spilled out of the cracked mirror, which Sookie had set on the ground. It surrounded my sister like a cloak, swirling and thrashing in the wind and making Sookie's face appear harsh and forbidding.

She had a burning stick that she used to ignite something she was holding in her other hand. I squinted and recognized it as the hemlock we had found at the creek. Why had she kept it, knowing it was a witch's evil plant? As if to answer my question, her voice rang out, piercing my ears.

"With this burnt offering, let my magic move beyond the abyss. *Oscail-an-doras!*"

Like brushfire, the light jumped from the mirror toward my sister and then toward the door in the center of the circle. Swirling light illuminated the door and it opened with a thundering crack.

Then I heard the most bloodcurdling sound of all.

Howls ripped through the air and my jaw dropped as four black, lumbering fiends sprang from the door. Their yellow eyes glowed like jack-o'-lanterns and steam curled from their snapping jaws.

Sookie had unleashed the hounds of hell.

CHAPTER 25

A Fiendish Bargain

FROZEN, WE WATCHED in horror as the slavering fiends lurched toward the forest. The criminals screamed in high-pitched voices as they pointed their guns at the beasts, firing uselessly, only to drop their guns and run when the fiends closed in.

"*Waheela*," Amanda gasped, as she watched the black bog creatures chase after the men, the fiends' powerful jaws foaming in anticipation. "Those *waheela* are going to bite off their heads," she said in horror.

I stared helplessly as the forest swallowed up the men and the fiends. My heart pounded in my ears through each terrifying second. The fiends' howls grew distant and then died off. At the same time, the winds died down too, and the ash and dirt settled in thick clouds around the medicine wheel. Finally, Sookie stopped her eerie chanting, extinguishing the light that had been streaming out of the fairy mirror.

I released a ragged breath. For a while, there was heavy silence. Until ...

"So, those fiends are gone for good, right?" Mia asked nervously. I assumed she meant both kinds of fiends – the human kind and the creatures of the bog.

Sookie didn't answer. Instead she was staring into the

fairy mirror with a puzzled expression. She looked up at me and her face was flushed. "I wasn't expecting that."

I had heard Sookie say that before ... and it was never good news.

Utterly exhausted, I slumped to the ground, unable to think of what to do next. The earth beneath me began to buzz, but I had no energy left to check where it was coming from. Everyone else had sat down too, except Sookie and Skeeter. He was looking over my sister's shoulder, staring curiously at the mirror. "How'd you do that?" he asked.

Sookie shook her head weakly. She now resembled her nine-year-old self instead of the powerful magician she'd become just moments ago. I refused to use the *W*-word.

"Ow," complained Jasper as he shoved his grimy fingers into his eyes and pulled out his contact lenses. "There's so much dirt and ash in my eyes, I can't bear these things anymore. I'm good as blind now."

"I guess your spare glasses are ..." I began.

"Ash, along with all my books," Jasper grumbled.

Amarjeet folded her knees under her chin and rocked herself, while Mia leaned against Mitch. Skeeter practically crawled into Clive's lap. Jasper stretched out with his arm over his face. My friends were pretty much spent. I went over to where Sookie had sat down alone, but she shrugged me away when I tried to put an arm around her. She seemed ... I had to search for the word ... inconsolable. But why did she look so unbearably sad? We'd gotten rid of the crooks and there was no sign of the fiends. Maybe she was just exhausted like the rest of us.

The lingering sun streaked the sky red. The temperature should have plunged as the sun set, but it remained strangely warm inside the circle. Feeling the exhaustion of the day, and with the warmth enveloping me like a blanket, I stretched out like Jasper and finally fell into a deep sleep for the first time in days.

I was in an amusement park. It wasn't like the one in Sweden. It was smaller, more like a carnival, and I was sitting on a garishly painted carousel horse that spun round and round.

I didn't like these merry-go-round horses. These weren't painted ponies like the horses I had usually seen in carousels. Under their bridles, they had bared sharp, yellow fangs, and their ghostly eyes reminded me of the fiends. Faster and faster the horses spun, while the calliope cranked out a tune that sounded like organ music from old black-and-white horror shows.

"I want to get off," I cried.

"There's no getting off," said Great Aunt Hildegaard. "You have to stay until your ride is finished." I looked over and saw that she was riding the horse beside me. I watched my aunt morph into the wild-eyed fortune-teller I'd met in Sweden.

"Child, you are doomed," she said in a hollow voice, her eyes narrow slits of white. "The fates have turned against you and each time you succeed worse will wait."

I woke up with a gasp and looked around. I shuddered. It's not fun to wake up from a nightmare and find out your real-life situation is even worse. It was still dark, but inside the circle where we slept the air around us glowed softly.

We must have been asleep for hours. Everyone was still passed out on the ground. Everyone, that is, except Sookie. I looked around, finally spotting her sitting alone under a nearby tree just outside the circle. She was staring into the fairy mirror. Part of me, the part that was maybe getting too used to my sister's magic, hoped she'd made contact through the mirror and we would be rescued soon.

"What do you see?" I asked quietly, joining her next to the tree.

Sookie looked up and I could tell by her tear-streaked cheeks that she was really upset. I crouched down beside her. "What's wrong?"

"Don't be angry, Cat."

"What do you mean?" I said this kind of sharply because fright had taken hold of me.

"I had to make a promise."

"What kind of promise?" These words came out slowly, as if I were still dreaming.

"I had to make a deal with a fairy," she finished in a whisper.

CHAPTER 26

A Secret Door

MY HEART THUDDED in my ears. "Why would you make a fairy deal, Sookie? You know those kinds of bargains end in disaster."

"It's only a little promise but ..."

"No such thing," I said. "What was it?"

"Just that I had to finish what I started. If I opened the door to magic, I had to remember to shut it."

That didn't sound so bad – actually it sounded like a good idea. But fairy deals were often treacherous. I didn't like this one bit. "Why didn't you tell me before?"

"I *told* you I had to summon help from the fairy mirror," Sookie said. "Where did you think the help would come from?"

I hadn't thought about that. I only knew that we'd have no chance unless my sister used her magic. *Come on, Cat,* said a miserable voice inside me. *No matter what, you knew if your sister used her magic there'd be a cost.* "If it was only a little promise, why are you upset?"

"I'm not. I ... was just homesick."

Even though that made sense, I still worried. But Sookie stubbornly refused to say anything more. All I managed to do was wake up the others by my attempts to get her to talk.

"What's wrong?" asked Jasper.

"Are those men back?" Clive looked around in alarm. "Or the hell hounds?" He got a panicked look and slapped his forehead. "Right, I should have thought of it first. Mitch, wake up and help me gather up the guns!"

Mitch shot up in a flash. While Mitch and Clive went to gather the guns the outlaws had dropped, I quickly told Jasper what Sookie had said.

"What does that mean, shutting the door to magic?" asked Jasper.

"I'm not exactly sure. I just know it was a promise," said Sookie. "In exchange for summoning help. I'll know when the time comes what I'm supposed to do." Then Sookie's eyes grew watery as she blinked back tears. "I didn't know the help would be those black wolves. They scare me, Cat. And ... and I *don't* know what I'll be asked to do."

I gave my sister a reassuring hug. She was half-frozen, so I brought her back inside the warmth of the medicine wheel before questioning her more. Once she'd settled in, I turned to her and frowned. "Who is giving you these so-called instructions?" I asked, suddenly suspicious. "Who have you been talking to in the mirror? It's not Lea, is it?"

Sookie's expression grew more guarded and she pulled away from me. "It's a secret," she mumbled.

"Not anymore," I demanded. "Tell me who you've been talking to."

Sookie shut down and got that stubborn look. This was just great, not only did she not know exactly what she'd promised, but she refused to tell me who she'd promised it to. How was I supposed to help if she wouldn't talk to me? Annoyed, I played the older sister card. "Tell me," I demanded. "Now."

"You're not the boss of everyone," Sookie said to me. But she didn't say that in her usual obstinate tone. Her words were so full of sorrow, they left a shadow on my heart. What did she mean?

Then it occurred to me. "You can't tell me, can you?" I said as a harsh memory surfaced. My friend Lea had been fairy-bound not to tell us anything about her evil aunt. It was as if a magic spell sewed her lips shut when she tried.

Sookie nodded miserably. "It was part of the deal," she muttered.

Uneasiness stole over me as the sun began to rise. As the sky turned pink, the medicine wheel pulsed a strange green light in the rhythm of a beating heart.

"What's going on?" I asked in alarm. The circle stones began shining like glow-in-the-dark skulls.

We all leaped away from the stones and stared in amazement. The hum grew louder until it sounded like a million mosquitoes were preparing to launch an attack. The early morning light gathered together into a burning ray that lit a fire along each spoke of the medicine wheel.

Amanda gasped. "It must be the summer solstice," she said. "My grandmother said that the medicine wheel became very important on the summer solstice because ..." She rubbed her temples. Her voice took on an exasperated tone. "I can't remember."

"Maybe I know," said Jasper. "Those hounds you

called *waheela* are the same supernatural beasts the Celts called bog fiends. The Dene pay close attention to the Otherworld just like the Celts did. Both people accepted the fairy world instead of pretending it didn't exist."

Amanda nodded in agreement.

Jasper paused and gave me a sober look. "You're not going to like this next bit, Cat."

I was one step ahead of him. "Let me guess now," I said. "The summer solstice is like the winter solstice, a time when our two worlds overlap."

Looking miserably at the heap of ashes that used to be the cabin, Jasper said, "If only I had my books." He drew a breath. "So this part is a stretch, but I think it's possible that during the solstice the medicine wheel becomes a door to the Otherworld."

Could this be the door that Sookie had to shut?

There was something Jasper was missing – that spooky loft – how did that haunted place fit into the equation? I had a hunch, a nasty intuition, that the loft played into this in some way.

Before I could pursue that thought, the outer circle of the medicine wheel caught on fire. And then the center of the medicine circle lit up like a candle, shooting flames into the sky. The fire had no effect on the door, which swung open in a loud whoosh of air.

CHAPTER 27

A Ghastly Sacrifice

BLUE, GREEN, AND scarlet flames spilled from the open door inside the medicine circle. That fire was too unusual to be from our world. Also, it was blinding, making it impossible to see beyond the flames to inside the door. The outer circle began rotating like a wheel, reminding me of the carousel in my nightmare.

The air around us began gyrating and had the same effect as when we'd opened the loft door. It tugged at our hair, our clothes, and even our skin.

"Back away from the circle!" I screamed at the top of my lungs, but the roaring rush of wind drowned my voice.

We stumbled away from the medicine wheel and gathered at the edge of the forest. The charred ruins of the cabin lifted up and spiraled into the open doorway, swirling like water going down a drain before disappearing into whatever was on the other side of that door. The wind ripped leaves off the trees and they spun into the opening too. Whole bushes were yanked up by their roots and they flew into the door's gaping maw. As soon as anything flew in, blue light streamed out, growing stronger and more menacing.

We backed farther into the forest, but it didn't help. Branches began snapping around us. Everything that could come loose got sucked into the spiraling vortex that was building in front of the door. We tried to keep moving, but the tug of the wind was too strong. I grabbed Sookie's hand and with my other arm anchored us to a stout tree trunk.

"It's like a black hole," screamed Clive, who kept a firm grip on Skeeter's jacket while holding on tightly to the tree trunk beside us.

"A hole where nothing escapes, not even planets," I said. That had popped out of my mouth unexpectedly, a snag of memory from one of Ms. Dreeble's science lectures.

"It's not going to swallow the planet," Clive yelled back. Then he closed his mouth in horror as he watched the trees closest to the medicine wheel shoot like javelins toward the open door and then get sucked inside. Even the ground became gouged and pockmarked as chunks of dirt flew into the chaos.

"Aaaoooooo!" Howls echoed in the wind. My eyes almost popped out of my head as the fiends, all four of them, flew past us, flapping their legs like giant demented bats. They too disappeared inside the swirling vortex.

I knew it would only be a matter of moments before the same thing happened to us.

"My magic did this," Sookie said. "I opened the door. I ... I ... know what I have to do now."

Then she let go of my hand.

"Sookie!" I screamed.

I watched my sister move toward the circle, except that unlike everything else, her feet remained on the ground while the vortex pulled her toward the open door.

I let go of the tree that I'd been clinging to for dear

life. The wind pulled me forward and I felt as if I were skiing downhill because, no matter which direction I pointed myself, I began sliding in the dirt. As I closed in on the stone circle, I felt my body lifting in the air. And then I fell back to the ground as something anchored me.

I looked down and saw Clive holding on to me like a crazy person. I began kicking, trying to break free of his arms.

"Are you insane?" he cried out.

"Are you?" I shot back. "Keep yourself safe. I have to get my sister." Our shouts were whispers in the deafening screech of the wind.

"We'll get her together," yelled Clive. "Somehow."

But we didn't have time to argue anymore. The vortex was pulling us in. Our bodies lifted and became airborne. I flapped my arms foolishly as if I could steer – but nothing helped as I spun toward the circle. Up and up we rose, until I was too terrified to think about the medicine wheel, the secret door, or even my little sister. I counted down the seconds until I would crash to my death like a plane in a graveyard spin.

One minute Clive and I were being tossed around like kites and the next minute we were drifting downward, landing on all fours on the soft dirt below. I slammed my chin against a medicine stone that peered up at me like a laughing skull. I rubbed the bruise and tried to take in what was happening.

The blue light pouring from the door had dimmed and the hurricane winds had almost died down too. It took a couple of seconds for my brain to catch up to what my eyes were seeing.

The door was almost shut, but it remained open a crack, just enough to reveal Sookie – standing inside. She was bathed in a bright white light that outlined her body, making her appear ghostly. I gasped when I noticed the white raven perched upon her shoulder staring calmly at me.

"It's up to me to close the door," said Sookie. "That's my part of the bargain. This is what I *have* to do."

"No, Sookie, no," I cried, breaking into a run.

But Sookie had already started to swing the door inward.

"It's okay, Cat," my little sister said. "Remember what you said? It's my turn to make a sacrifice."

She uttered the Celtic words that I knew too well: *"Bear-leat-an-leanbh." Take the child.*

And then the door slammed shut.

CHAPTER 28
Dark Whispers

I SCREAMED AND ran for the door, clawing at the handle. When it wouldn't budge, I pounded my fists against it. "Help me!" I cried.

Clive ran to my side and kicked at the door, and we were soon joined by the others. Skeeter cried miserably while he banged on the door and yelled for Sookie to come out.

The door groaned and then a strange rumble filled the air, but I paid no attention. I had only one goal in mind – to open that door and get my sister out. But even though I fought them wildly, my friends dragged me away just as the door tumbled forward and slammed heavily against the earth.

There was only air on the other side. No light, not a hint of the Otherworld. With aching hands, I began beating the wood, and when that didn't work, I leaned over and yanked and yanked. Still, the door didn't budge. Again, arms pulled me away. Jasper and Clive patted me on the back, trying to comfort me, while Amarjeet stroked my hair. Slowly my screams turned to cries and then into miserable sobs.

* * *

The sun warmed my shoulders as it reached its highest peak in the sky. I was hunched against the ground, my arm stretched pathetically across the door. For the last several hours, I'd been in a stupor – neither conscious nor folded into the comforting arms of sleep.

My eyes were almost swollen shut and my throat ached unbearably. Occasionally, Jasper, Clive, or Amarjeet crept over and tried to talk to me. I pushed them away, and they'd leave me alone for a while before someone else came over to check on me again.

The flu felt better than this. Everything ached – my head, my body, and especially my heart. What had happened to Sookie? Where had she gone? Those lonely thoughts rattled around in my head.

"Did you hear that?" asked Mia.

"Could you be more specific?" Clive retorted.

"That," she pronounced again. Then she pointed toward the sky. "Oh my god."

The whirr of helicopter blades grew louder as the red body of a rescue helicopter came into view. My friends jumped up and down, waving their arms like maniacs and screeching with glee. I turned my heavy head skyward, holding a hand over my eyes, shading them from the sun's hurtful glare. One – no, two helicopters swept over us and hovered over the small clearing.

"Step away," a loud voice commanded through a speaker. "Then we can land."

Dirt swept up and leaves fluttered as the helicopters landed where the cabin had once sat. A man and a woman in paramedic uniforms emerged from the helicopters, checking us over, quietly reassuring us that we'd be fine. As if they knew anything about what had happened. The woman stood with her hands on her hips and said, "Aren't you lot a sorry looking mess?" Then she smiled. "But you managed better than some of the most experienced hikers. Three nights in this wilderness is no place for amateurs. You all must have excellent survival skills."

Her praise was lost on me. I simply stumbled along – moving my legs, then sitting down in the helicopter seat. I snapped my seat belt together robotically. I might as well have been a zombie.

"Your friends said this is yours." The woman handed me my backpack.

I grabbed it without saying a word. The bag had torn and the fairy mirror winked at me. I reached in, ready to pitch it out onto the ground before we took off, but some urge stopped my hand. A strange fragment of my dream resurfaced and I could hear my Great Aunt Hildegaard saying, "Not until the ride is over, Cat." I shoved the stupid mirror back inside my pack and clutched the bag to my chest.

That's the position I remained in for the entire ride. We landed in the closest town, which was so small it didn't even have a hospital, so instead we were ushered into a local medical clinic. While they'd given us loads of water to drink on the helicopter, we weren't allowed to eat until the doctor checked us over.

"Some minor burns on your arms and face, and your chin also took a nasty bump," said a woman in a white lab coat. She wrapped my arm in a sling. "Keep this on for a day to take the stress off your shoulder. Drink lots and your throat will feel better. You might try apple juice."

She handed me a jar of salve and ushered Amarjeet inside. I sat down on the bench outside the clinic.

The woman from the helicopter came over to talk to us while we were waiting. "Your parents have all been notified that you've been rescued. We're going to keep you here in town tonight, just to make sure you're well enough to travel and the police will want to speak with you. Then we'll fly you to the city tomorrow. Your parents all wanted to meet you here, but we let them know that we've picked you up so far north that it would be faster for them to just wait in the city. There aren't even any flights into this town."

I nodded woodenly.

Amanda asked, "Did you find anyone else besides us in the woods?"

Her question felt like a stab. I hung my head.

The helicopter pilot laughed softly and said, "As a matter of fact, we've located three men who gave themselves up right away." She shook her head. "The police are sure they're your kidnappers. They were babbling about giant wolves and demonic children, though." She laughed again, but then a serious shadow crossed her face. "It's not the first time people have emerged from the forest with strange tales."

After the doctors were done checking us over, we all had a chance to speak to our parents on the phone. I waited until everyone else had finished talking before I punched in the number and took the receiver in my hand. Mom answered right away.

"Cat, are you all right?" Mom sounded breathless.

I began choking up.

"Are you hurt?"

"No, Mom," I managed to sputter as I swallowed back tears. I tried to tell her Sookie had disappeared, but I couldn't bring myself to say it. Finally the paramedic took the phone from my hand and reassured my mother I was fine.

A rescue worker took us to a restaurant beside the small clinic and I watched Mitch wolf down three burgers. The others weren't far behind him. I stared at my burger and fries.

"Poor thing," said the waitress. "I heard on the news about how all you kids got lost in Headless Valley. You've had too much of a shock."

She had no idea.

"Why don't I wrap that burger up for you to eat later? I'll get you some soup for now."

I sipped the soup to ease my sore throat. Jasper pinned me with a stare. "C'mon Cat, you've got to keep up your strength. We'll get Sookie back."

But I knew he had no more of an idea what had happened to her than I did. Just as I knew deep down that I wouldn't see her again.

* * *

The town's hotel was really only a house with several spare rooms. I collapsed on the bed while Mia and Amarjeet argued over who'd shower first. They left me alone and for once, Mia didn't complain when I woke her up with my sobs. I went into the bathroom to wash my face and blow my nose. I couldn't recognize the pathetic person that stared back at me from the bathroom mirror. My new tunic was filthy and snagged beyond repair. My leggings were ripped into tatters and not in a fashionable way. I winced, remembering the flash of anger I had felt when Sookie commented on this stupid outfit in front of my friends. What a dumb thing to be annoyed over. My eyes welled with more tears.

"Pssst, Cat."

I flinched. In the bathroom mirror, my eyes widened – I recognized that voice.

"Cat ..."

I flew out of the bathroom and cursed under my breath when I stubbed my toe on a chair.

"Sookie?" I cried out.

"Open up your backpack," ordered the muffled voice.

I scrambled in the dark until I found my pack. I yanked it open. A mystical light lit the dark room. The fairy mirror was glowing. I pulled it out and mist swirled in the looking glass.

"I'm here, Cat," the mirror said.

Chapter 29

Mirror Magic

MIA MUMBLED AND rolled over, pulling her pillow on top of her head. She must have still been asleep because she said, "Not you two again ..." clearly forgetting my sister had disappeared.

Amarjeet snored softly. I grabbed the fairy mirror and shut myself in the bathroom.

"Sookie?" I whispered urgently. I thought I'd lost my sister forever, but she was contacting me through the mirror somehow. Was I dreaming? Panicking, I pinched myself – hard. "Ow."

"Cat, I'm okay," said Sookie.

"Where are you?" If only the fog in the mirror would clear. I could hear Sookie, but I couldn't see her.

"I'm home, Cat."

"How is that possible?" But I knew that the Otherworld was a strange and mysterious place where maps and miles had no bearing. "Why can't I see anything in this mirror?"

"Hang on," my sister said. Gradually the mist lifted and I could see the outside of our house. My heart squeezed tight as I watched Mom throw a suitcase in the car.

"Mom won't wait until morning to drive into the city. I don't see the point myself," said Sookie. "It's not like you'll be there until tomorrow ..."

"*You* told the authorities where we were, didn't you?" I said.

"Yes, Cat."

"Thank you, Sookie."

The mirror began fogging up again as Mom ran back into our house.

"You sound a little strange," I said to my sister. "A kind of echo is making your voice lower."

"It's the mirror magic," explained Sookie. "I've got to go now. I'll see you soon."

"Wait," I called out. "How did you explain showing up in town without us?" But the glass in the mirror went dark.

Sookie was home. I said that to myself over and over. Each time I repeated it, my heart soared higher.

Suddenly I was overpowered with a terrible hunger. I went back to the room and unwrapped my burger, devouring it in three seconds and still feeling hungry when I was done. Mia and Amarjeet had brought cookies back to the room. I found them and began munching through oatmeal and then chocolate chip cookies, promising myself I'd replace them in the morning.

After I stuffed myself I went into the bathroom and prepared a hot bath, dumping a whole bottle of bath soap into the tub. Fragrant steam floated up as I slipped into the mass of bubbles, soaking each cut, bruise, and ache while I lathered soot and ash out of my hair.

I swear when I was done there was a ring in the bathtub as dark as ink. We'd each been given a set of clothes at the clinic. I shrugged on a long, clean T-shirt that had RESCUE written across the front and slipped into a baggy pair of navy jogging pants. Then I climbed into bed and drifted into the most blissful, warm sleep I'd ever had.

* * *

"Wake up." Someone tossed a pillow onto my stomach. "Snorf" was my strangled response.

"You've been asleep all morning. The police have arrived – they've flown in a special investigative team ..." Mia gave me a gentle shove. "Get up, Cat."

I sat up in bed and stretched languidly, enjoying each moment. So what if I had an advanced science exam to write, and so what if high school would be a big change? Life. Was. Good. I yawned.

"Did you eat our cookies?" asked Amarjeet.

I apologized to my friends for stealing their snacks and they said they'd let me off the hook as long as I hurried downstairs. We crowded inside the small office of the town's only constable. "Sookie was the one who told the authorities where to find us," I told Jasper proudly.

Jasper looked at me with concern while the others seemed confused. I guessed they didn't understand how things worked when you traveled fairy style. Come to think of it, I didn't know how she'd done it either.

"I ... I guess that makes sense," Mia said with a curious frown. The way she said that, I had the sudden feeling that we weren't talking about the same thing at all. I slid into a seat, and before I could puzzle it out, two detectives strode inside the office and sat behind a table the constable and his volunteer had set up.

We told our story as a group, beginning with the nightmare ride on the bus. "Yes, we'd escaped from the men twice, yes, there were wolves, big ones, and the last we saw of the robbers were their backs as they ran into the forest. No, none of us were hurt." We avoided all mention of magic mirrors, headless skeletons, and the door to the Otherworld. Come to think of it, I wasn't sure my friends even remembered any of that – nobody had asked a single question about how Sookie had returned to town. Even to me that part of the adventure was fading in memory like a long-forgotten soccer loss.

When we'd finished, the detectives asked all the others to step outside, except for Clive and me.

"Tell us again about the diamond conversation you overheard between the pilot and the bus driver," commanded the inspector. His gray hair was cut really short, and while his face seemed kindly, his eyes bore straight into ours.

Clive and I recounted the robbers' plan of salting the mines with stolen uncut diamonds.

The inspector shook his head. "You and your friends were in grave danger," he said. "This was an international plot with millions of dollars at stake. Investors from all over the world were waiting for the report on the diamond mines. Those men would have stopped at nothing to keep you quiet."

Even though I had already known that, I still gulped. Then I recalled the first bus driver, the neat freak. "Is our bus driver – the real one – okay?" My heart skipped a beat as I worried he might have been killed.

"He's all right – he was hit on the head and has a minor concussion, but he's conscious," said a younger, blond officer.

"He's not going to be happy when he sees his bus," Clive shook his head.

The blond woman smiled. "I think he'll be okay. He won't be held responsible. The gang involved in the smuggling operation had infiltrated the bus dispatch office. It was their plan from the start to use an unregistered bus for a getaway."

"But they got more than they bargained for, it appears," said the chief investigator.

He didn't know the half of it.

When the detectives were done, the hotel served us a huge breakfast and I almost broke Mitch's record by eating six pancakes. Afterwards, we boarded a small plane flown here especially for us, and I waited anxiously to take off. Twice during breakfast I had snuck away to check on my sister. Each time she reassured me she was fine, even though she could no longer get rid of that strange, magical mist from the mirror.

"I'm staying here," Amanda announced to our surprise. "My parents are driving north to meet me, so that I can see my grandmother. I called her last night and told her what happened." Amanda came up and held my arm lightly. "My granny said you are special, Cat. You are a spirit walker, one who can travel in both the human world and the spirit world at the same time."

For some weird reason my eyes misted up. It wasn't

every day that an adult or even one of my friends recognized that much more was going on in my life than most people would ever know. And maybe when I got back home, things would change. Maybe this time more of us would remember what we'd just survived. I felt the load I was always carrying around lighten. I nodded and told Amanda to thank her grandmother. The lore she'd taught Amanda had come in handy, and now Amanda and I were on better terms too.

"One more thing," Amanda called out as we climbed into the waiting van. "Granny says not to lose faith. You must fight the fates."

I shivered, remembering a fortune-teller had once told me something similar. That was peculiar. I didn't need to fight anything. I was perfectly happy with how everything turned out. I shrugged my shoulders, smiled, and waved goodbye.

* * *

Mom was at the airport and I swear her arms were opened wide long before the plane even landed. After she had squeezed all the air from my lungs, she finally let me go and I noticed for the first time that the waiting area was packed. I did a double take and rubbed my eyes. Mr. Morrows and Ms. Dreeble had come to greet us. I sure didn't see that coming.

Mr. and Mrs. Singh were there and so were Jasper's parents, Mr. and Mrs. Chung. Even Mia's mom was there – she had canceled her hospital shift. Mitch's father looked worse than we did, and only Mitch could have survived his crushing hug. Clive and Skeeter looked around for their grandmother.

"Your grandmother wanted to be here," my mom said to them, "but her back was acting up. I told her I'd be happy to drop you two off." Clive nodded stoically as he put his arm around Skeeter. My heart tugged when I saw how alone he looked.

"Where's Sookie, Mom?" But Mom wasn't paying any attention – she was helping Skeeter hoist up his pants, since he kept tripping over the oversized pair the rescue team had given him. I wondered if Alice Greystone was keeping an eye on Sookie. I knew her sister, Lucinda, had become too frail to travel. When I thought of her failing health, a dart of sorrow stung me and I remembered how unfair it was that the fairies had robbed her of most of her life. Lucinda had been trapped in a fairy circle at my age and released as a little old lady years later, even though to her it only felt like days had passed. I couldn't imagine anything worse.

I could see how Sookie would be too tuckered out to travel into the city. My friends and I could hardly keep our heads up and eyes open. Despite a full night's sleep, we were physically exhausted. Mr. Morrows shook all of our hands and blathered on about how proud he was that we remembered there was no "I" in team. Whatever that meant. Ms. Dreeble gave us all hugs and then had to wipe her glasses because they kept steaming up.

Clive, Skeeter, and I stumbled to the car, and Mom had to help Skeeter snap his seatbelt shut because he was already out cold by the time he sat down. Clive and I dozed most of the way home.

As we crossed the bridge into town, I felt that moth-like feeling flutter inside my stomach again. I shivered even though it was a sunny day in June.

That chill morphed to cold dread when we drove into town.

CHAPTER 30

A Dreadful Homecoming

SOMETHING WASN'T RIGHT. For one thing, when we drove down the main street, many of the shops had their shades pulled down even though it was midday. Even Mr. Keating had his apple barrels tucked inside the store instead of out on his porch, and the window shutters of the Emporium were closed, though I saw people walking in and out.

When we drove down the side streets, I saw that all the houses had their curtains drawn and their porch lights on even though it was daytime. So odd – I was reminded of someplace else, but my brain was still fogged from exhaustion and I couldn't put my finger on where it was. I scratched the white scar on my arm – the scar left by a fairy thorn. Ever since we drove into town it had been itching like crazy.

We pulled up in front of Clive and Skeeter's house. The lawn was neatly trimmed and the porch swept clean, although it needed to be painted and a broken window upstairs had cardboard taped to it.

Skeeter could barely be woken, so Mom carried him to the porch. Clive's grandmother opened the door before Mom could knock. She thanked my mother repeatedly and hugged Skeeter, even though he was asleep and barely stood upright when Mom set him down. Clive undid his seatbelt, but instead of joining his grandmother and brother, he slid next to me into the driver's seat Mom had just vacated.

"I just wanted to say," Clive began awkwardly, "that ... well, you're better than anyone I know at almost everything." Then he added with only a ghost of a smirk, "Except maybe at social studies." Clive grabbed my hand and held it.

Had the world ended? Clive hadn't even backhanded his compliment by saying " ... better for a *girl*." I had to bite back my usual flippant answer. This was unexpected.

I was surprised to find that Clive's hand wasn't sweaty but cool, smooth, and firm. And my hand felt comfortable enclosed in his. How could I have even considered sitting beside Zach at the cafeteria lunch table or hanging out with him at the lockers? Sure he was popular and nice, but it was Clive who had my back. Clive was the boy who drove me crazy, the boy who challenged everyone – especially me. But he always stood up for what he thought was right. And I could always count on him in a disaster.

As if he read my mind, he said, "I just wanted to say thanks for keeping your head and not panicking, and thanks for," Clive stumbled through the next part, "thanks for, um, well ... being reliable in a crisis."

A shadow crossed Clive's face. It was a look I recognized – Jasper sometimes still had it when he gazed at Mia. "I only wish I could rely on your heart." He released my hand. I let it hang there, not knowing what to do. But inside my head, I was shouting to myself, "Clive thinks you don't care for him. Do something!"

"Clive, I know you've been through a trying time, but have you forgotten your manners?" Clive's grandmother called out to us. "Come and help Mrs. Peters with Skeeter. He needs to be carried to bed."

Clive jumped out of the car and before I could say anything, he was gone.

I had only just figured out which boy I cared for most and lost my chance to do something about it a second later. But Clive was right – my heart wasn't reliable. First I liked Zach, then I got all confused about Zach, then I got all confused about Clive. Now it was clear that Clive *was* special to me. But was it wrong that I'd needed time to decide who I wanted to be with?

As we drove the last blocks to our house, Mom leaned over and patted my shoulder. "You're done in, aren't you, sweetie? You've hardly said a word."

"I just want to get home and crawl into my own bed."

When we turned down our street, I saw Jasper and his family. I rolled down my window and waved. Jasper waved back, but only halfheartedly. His face seemed troubled. That's when I noticed curious music drifting from the river. Trepidation rode up and down my arms and neck as if I were lying on a bed of pins. It was a calliope and I swear it was pumping out the creepy music that I had heard in my dream.

"Do you hear that?" I asked nervously.

"Do you mean the carnival music?" Mom pulled into our driveway.

"Carnival?" Fever chills spread over my skin.

"The carnival pulled into town last night. You can go this afternoon if you'd like." Mom smiled.

"I'm too tired." I shook my head. But something told me I had to go, to see if it looked like the carnival in my nightmare. "Maybe my friends would like to go tonight."

"Not at night!" Mom snapped as she turned off the car. "No children are allowed out at night. It isn't safe!"

I stared at my mother. What was she talking about? Then I remembered the image Sookie had shown me in the fairy mirror, of Mom at her wit's end. "Okay," I said quietly. "I'll wait." I desperately hoped she'd move on from this overprotective streak soon.

I got out of the car and my jaw dropped as several trucks passed by and swung onto the narrow road leading to the top of Grim Hill. "What's going on?" I asked. The road had been overgrown since Halloween, but I noticed now that the trees had been trimmed since I had been gone. No one ever went up the hill since we'd closed down Grimoire School. Since then Grim Hill was considered haunted and had become as deserted as a place could be. No wonder Jasper looked freaked.

"Mom," I said in a shaky voice. "What's going on at Grim Hill?"

"Oh, I forgot to tell you my big news," Mom said, her eyes twinkling with excitement. "They're building a posh new private school on top of that hill and guess who they've hired as the new school secretary? I can ditch the night school courses with the wonderful salary they'll pay."

This couldn't be happening. I shook myself. I was still

stuck in Headless Valley, delirious without food and water. This was some kind of hallucination. *Just a coincidence, Cat,* I told myself. Just because you know there's magic doesn't mean everything is magical. It could be a regular school.

Still, it didn't help when Mom said, "Maybe there will be tuition cuts for children of staff. And you could attend."

My heart slammed against my chest. She'd uttered similar words back at Halloween, when she'd been under a diabolical spell. *Coincidence, Cat.* I breathed and shook it off. "Let's go inside. I can't wait to give Sookie a great big hug."

"Wait," Mom said sharply. Her eyes crinkled as she frowned. "Cat, you know how I've always told you to be fair-minded and kind to everyone."

I nodded.

"And it's true we have a certain obligation. After all, Sookie alerted the authorities about where you were."

Where was Mom going with this? I nodded again.

"So I want you to try hard and understand because I'm going to make this extremely clear."

Mom drew in a short breath and exhaled slowly. "Under no circumstances are you to have any contact with Sookie. I'm sorry, but I don't want you mixing with her kind."

CHAPTER 31

An Unsettling Mystery

BLOOD RACED THROUGH my veins so fast it pounded in my ears. I'd been through a lot – of course, that was it. Maybe I was in shock and I'd misheard my own mother telling me not to go near Sookie.

"Mom, why are you telling me I can't see my own sister?" I expected her to laugh, and say, "Good heavens, Cat, what on earth do you think I said?"

Except she didn't – instead, she placed her hand on my forehead and stared into my eyes. "I don't like that bruise on your chin. Maybe you also hit your head. I'm going to get our family doctor to check on you."

"No, Mom, I'm fine. I just don't understand what you're telling me."

"I'm telling you," her voice dropped to a whisper and she checked over her shoulder as if she was afraid of being overheard. "You *must* stay away from Sookie. You know perfectly well that there are some things in this town that we just don't speak about."

Trucks filled with building material lumbered past us. The carnival's calliope music caterwauled eerie tunes in the background. The scent of fresh lavender and jasmine drifted from our yard – shrubs that Sookie had planted. Why, then, did nothing seem real?

I ran to our door and waited impatiently for Mom to unlock it. Then I flew up the stairs and into my sister's room. It had disappeared! Not the room – that was still there. Only now it had been converted into a sewing room. Bolts of blue and purple silk lay by Mom's sewing machine. She'd dragged that creepy seamstress mannequin from the attic and it now looked like a giant voodoo doll, pinned with a blouse she'd been making me for high school.

There was no big Sookie mess, no tossed bed covers, no art pencils, no glitter pens, no pet hamster! Horror filled me – I'd been through this before, last fall, when Lucinda had taken my sister to Fairy. Sookie had been erased from everyone's minds as if she'd never existed.

What did you think, Cat? Your sister stepped through a fairy door to the Otherworld. Of course something happened. Something strange and terrible. Fairy bargains always come with a price.

Of course. You could practically taste the magic in the air. That's why your scar was acting up. Sure enough – when I checked the feather fastened to my waist, it didn't even pretend to be white. It glowed green and blue, then orange and red.

But something was different this time. I rubbed my aching arm and tried to figure it out. It wasn't as if Sookie didn't exist. Mom said she did, just that I wasn't allowed to see her. I went inside my room and ripped open my backpack. Grabbing the fairy mirror, I practically shouted into the looking glass. "Sookie! What happened?"

For a long time, the mist didn't clear. "Sookie," I

demanded. "Where are you? You know I won't give up until we speak."

The mirror still didn't clear up, but Sookie finally responded. "It's okay, Cat."

"Not likely," I shot back.

"I mean, I'm okay."

"Where are you?" Was she in Fairy? If she was, how would my mom know that? Things weren't adding up.

"Cat, it's better if we don't meet up yet. I need you to stay away." Then the mirror blackened – the mystical light behind it had winked out.

Right. Well, that simplified things. I changed into my jeans, clean sneakers, and a hoodie, and flew back down the stairs.

"Where are you going?" Mom asked suspiciously. "I thought you were exhausted."

"Second wind," I smiled sweetly. "I'm going to call on Jasper and check out the carnival."

Mom frowned. "I don't think you're up to ..."

"I'll be back nice and early," I promised. "Long before sunset, that way I'll turn in early and get a proper night's sleep."

"But you haven't eaten yet, Cat," Mom said. "I was fixing you a lunch. I don't want you filling up on carnival food."

"I ate a ton of pancakes for breakfast," I said, backing out the door. "I'm good until dinner. No junk food, I promise."

Before she could protest, I was leaping over our fence and racing through Jasper's yard.

He had the door open even before I hit the final step. "Something's not right, Cat," he said. Then fear stole across his face as he watched another truck drive past his house and turn up Grim Hill.

"I know where we have to go," I said.

Chapter 32
Carnival of Horrors

I TOLD JASPER about my mom's bizarre behavior. Jasper nodded and said, "When I was telling my parents about what had happened, and how Sookie rescued us, my mom acted as if she was having a heart attack."

"Let me guess," I jumped in. "Your parents told you not to go near Sookie."

Jasper pushed his old pair of glasses on top of his head. "It wasn't just that. It was their expressions." He stared at me. "Cat, they were terrified."

"We have to check out the carnival," I'd already leaped down the steps. "I had this dream – a nightmare – when we were in Headless Valley. It was of a carnival. I've a hunch we might find Sookie there."

Jasper grabbed a sweater and we were both off and running. We made it to the creek in half our usual time. When we arrived at the carnival, we slammed to a stop. My eyes could barely take in the scene in front of me. The riverbank was lined with booths painted garishly in purple and orange or red and lime green. The eerie carousel from my dream stood in the center. Odd-looking people that I didn't recognize wandered the carnival grounds. Jasper and I ducked behind a tent, staring in horror as two girls walked by – tall, slim, and shining with a haunting beauty that was marred by their cruel eyes and wicked smiles. They wore black and orange pinstripe Grimoire uniforms.

"Do you think they are fairies?" I gasped.

"Yes" was Jasper's strangled reply.

Old-fashioned tents flying strange banners festooned the midway. Some booths flew flags displaying mysterious runes. We wound our way through the maze of tents and booths, where peculiar looking vendors with odd colored eyes and thin pointed faces sold their wares, which weren't your ordinary fair prizes like stuffed alligators and plastic aliens. On the booth shelves sat creepy little dolls, the kind seen in horror shows, with china heads and nasty glass eyes that followed our every move. One booth contained puppets that danced on top of booth counters without any strings. Rattling wind chimes tapped out haunting tunes, and a heavy scent wafted from a tent selling diabolical plants. I recognized them from Sookie's magical garden – wolfsbane and Spanish moss, mandrake root and yew.

This wasn't any ordinary carnival. We didn't need our feathers to tell us that our town had fallen under a sinister enchantment. Magic was thick in the air.

We summoned our courage and checked every tent and booth for Sookie. But we needn't have worried. None of the fairy folk were interested in us. It was as if they thought they had nothing to fear from a couple of fairy fighters. "My sister's not here," I said in disappointment. "We may as well go."

"Yeah," agreed Jasper. "I don't want to stay any

longer than I have to."

As we left the carnival ground, a thick fog rolled in from the creek. It followed us as we walked down the neighborhood streets. That's when it hit me. The fog, the closed curtains, and pulled shades on Main Street – the fearful look in the townspeople's eyes. I'd witnessed all that before when we'd visited the town of Blakulla in Sweden.

"Jasper," I gasped. "I think Grim Hill is infested ..."

"With witches," Jasper's voice was filled with dread. "I sensed it as soon as my parents pulled into town." He hung his head. "But I didn't want to admit it, not even to myself."

I realized that everything I'd fought for over the past year had been undone – no, not just undone, made ten times worse! But how?

There was only one place we could go for help. Even though we were pretty much running on empty, Jasper and I raced to the Greystones. Surely they would know what was happening. Maybe they'd even be able to tell me where Sookie was.

Again, we ran through silent streets. Yellow fog floated through alleys, stretching its ghostly arms and causing the occasional people we spotted to scurry away to their homes. We stopped in front of the gate with the rusty hinge and the old-fashioned house with the wraparound porch. Somehow, even just seeing this place filled my heart with hope.

I banged on the brass doorknocker. A shade pulled open and Alice Greystone peeked out the window. She opened the door and invited us in. "Oh my dears," she said, giving us each a hug.

"Is it Cat and Jasper?" asked a frail voice from the living room.

"Yes," announced Alice Greystone, ushering us into their front parlor.

Lucinda sat on a camel-back velvet couch, a china tea cup resting on a doily on the dark table beside her. A pale blue quilt covered her lap and her skin looked even more translucent than I remembered. It was as if she were hardly in this world anymore. "Come sit beside me," she beckoned.

I sat down carefully, not wanting to give her a jolt. She took my hand in hers and I noticed how papery her skin felt.

"So you've both seen," Lucinda said.

Then the dam burst inside me and I blurted out the story of our whole adventure and our curious return. What I left out, Jasper filled in. Alice bustled in and out of the room bringing a plate of biscuits and a jug of lemonade, but nobody touched anything.

I shook my head in despair. "What happened?"

Lucinda spent most of her life in a fairy circle, so she was immune to the wicked glamour that fairies used to trick people's minds. She fastened me with eyes that brimmed with both sorrow and kindness.

"I fear that your sister opened the door to the Otherworld." Her tone sounded like Mom's when she'd told me the bad news of the divorce, so I knew Lucinda was keeping her voice steady for my sake while holding back her own misery.

"Once the door became unlocked, Fairy slipped

through. If only the door hadn't been opened on the summer solstice," Lucinda explained. "The Otherworld and our world were just too close."

"It's my fault." I bit my lip hard, trying not to break down. "I told Sookie to use her magic and summon help."

Alice Greystone came over and put her arm around me. "It's not your fault. You did what you had to do," she said firmly.

"We had no choice," Jasper agreed. "We'd have all been lost for sure."

"Sometimes one is forced to make a difficult choice," Lucinda's soft voice affirmed. "And it's not possible to predict the future."

But I can, I thought suddenly. I told Jasper and the Greystone sisters about my dream of the wicked carnival and that it was not the first time I had dreamt of the future. It had been a warning.

Lucinda considered this quietly. "Fairy time is like an elastic band," Lucinda said slowly. "It can snap backward and forward, which has considerable consequences for mortals."

She had that right, considering she'd aged seventy years in seven days.

"For one thing," said Lucinda. "You two have only been gone days, but it's been several weeks since the witch has taken over the town."

Witches! I knew it. Jasper let out a slow whistle.

"Maybe," Lucinda glanced at me quizzically, "maybe you have a gift, Cat. It seems you can see snippets of this fairy time. There must be a reason for that. We need to research this and help you with it. It might be important."

I hoped so, because as far as special powers go, mine had been useless so far.

There was one thing that couldn't wait. "Sookie," I said. "Do you know anything about Sookie?"

Alice frowned and Lucinda's expression grew uncomfortable.

"Where is she?" I demanded. "Is she hurt?"

"No, Cat," said Lucinda. "Sookie is unharmed."

"Then tell me where she is."

"At the old house by the cemetery," Lucinda revealed with reluctance.

Bea and Lea's old home. How could my Mom or anybody let a little girl live there by herself, unless – "She's not with Bea, is she?" I said in alarm.

"As far as I know, she's on her own," said Alice.

This wasn't making any sense. Before they could say anything more, I got up and ran out the door.

"Stop," called Alice. "We need to tell you more."

"Cat, wait for me," cried Jasper.

I kept running.

Chapter 33

An Uncertain Future

I PRACTICALLY FLEW to Lea's old home. I hated that place by the graveyard, with its haunted old house and sinister trees. When I reached the front yard, it became clear it was inhabited again. Half-drawn curtains revealed a guttering candle casting ghastly silhouettes against the window.

Bundles of strange dried plants hung from the front porch ceiling and I sneezed twice at the cloying odor of dark spice and wilted, dying roses. Wicked plants grew in thorny clusters along the cracked stone sidewalk. The whole house was caught in the chilling shadow of Grim Hill and I hesitated to march up to the front door. I decided to check around back instead.

The back garden had been restored to all of its creepy glory with monstrous potted plants that looked as if they might make a grab for me if I got too near. On the porch, a tall broom sat beside the backdoor. A very unfriendly black cat lazed in the weak sunlight, but sprang and hissed when I made it to the top of the steps. Something was very wrong with this place. I would have left had I not spotted the tiny troll doll placed on top of the banister.

Sookie had bought that ugly doll in Sweden.

I swallowed, then used the front of my sleeve to rub

away the dirt caked on a partly opened kitchen window and peered inside. The kitchen shelves and counter were crowded with jars stuffed with cuttings of peculiar plants and strange colored bulbs. A huge black cauldron sat on top of the stove and a foul green liquid threatened to bubble over.

The broom, the cat, the cauldron, and the herbs – this is where the witch lived. And she had Sookie! A screeching bird startled me. My heart hammered even louder when I noticed a white raven perched on a corner stand in the kitchen. It arched its ivory wings and fastened me with a beady black eye.

"*Caw! Hello!*" the bird screeched.

A tall blond woman wearing a long gray dress that could have been spun from spider silk swept into the kitchen. My heart sank. It was Bea, the wicked banshee who had tried to kill Jasper. That is, I thought it was Bea until she said ...

"Maeb, my sweet bird, who is there? Who dares come lurking at my door?"

The witch stared directly at me. Her glowing, cat-like eyes looked eerie – the irises were a familiar blue, but the pupils resembled black slits. And on her shoulder sat a hamster – Buddy!

This was the voice from the mirror that had comforted me in my darkest moments. Deeper, and somehow more powerful, but it was the same voice. I choked out the word that was already dying on my lips.

"Sookie?"

"Cat," the witch said. Warmth flashed across her face,

terribly out of place against her cold beauty.

"But how ...?" Backing away from the porch, I almost tumbled down the steps, but caught my footing and kept moving away. Sookie rushed to the door and flung it open.

"I've been in Fairy a long time," Sookie said to me. There was no sorrow in her voice when she said, "I've changed."

"You ... you're grown up. And you're a ... a witch," I sputtered from the yard.

"I'm afraid so, Cat." Sookie smiled ruefully, as if she were sorrier for me, now her sworn enemy, than for herself. "Remember, a sacrifice had to be made."

A memory of us sitting on the bus flashed through my mind. I recalled just how angry I had been when I was forced to take care of my sister. All she had wanted was to eat some snacks. "It's time you learned to sacrifice," I had told her. I began shivering as if I'd fallen into an icy lake.

I did the only thing I could do right now – I ran.

"Don't worry about me, Cat," Sookie called after me. "Now I can practice all the magic I want." Then she laughed wickedly. "It's truly fun."

I ran blindly and was out of breath by the time I'd run halfway up Grim Hill. I collapsed on the leaf-strewn ground. I don't know how long I sat there in a numbing daze, but it was now darker on the hill and the tree shadows had grown menacing. Strange squawks and groans came from the forest, sounds that no animal I was familiar with could have made.

Crunching footsteps signaled somebody's approach. I held my breath. "Cat?"

"Oh, Jasper," I cried.

Jasper burst through a copse of trees and joined me on the ground. "I followed you. I ... I saw Sookie." His voice was filled with sorrow.

I nodded, huddling on the ground in a heap of misery, pulling my knees to my chest. "What am I going to do?"

Jasper wasn't paying attention. He was looking over my shoulder and his eyes widened in surprise. "How ... how long has she been here?"

"A while," came the gentle voice. My heart skipped a beat when my friend Lea emerged from the shadows. There was a time when I thought all I wanted was to see her once more. How cruel fate was.

Fight the fates, a faint voice whispered in my ear.

"You know what happened?" I asked.

"Yes, Cat," Lea's red-rimmed eyes shed a tear. "Your mirror magic drew my attention back to Grim Hill. But I discovered what happened to your sister too late." The fairy girl seemed genuinely sad for me, which was unusual for her kind – to feel anything for mortals. But Lea had always been different.

"You know how Fairy works," I said suddenly. "There must be something I can do to fix this mess."

Lea's gentle features grew pinched and she tossed her red hair as she stared up the hill.

Determination burned inside me. This wasn't how things could end. I wouldn't let this happen. "Lea," I persisted. "What can I do to save my sister and take away the enchantment?"

"Maybe there is one way," Lea shook her head slowly.

"It's perilous. You're not going to like it, Cat."

I'd broken down when the secret door closed, trapping Sookie inside. Then I had collapsed in sorrow unable to do anything about it. I *refused* to go to that dark place again. This wasn't going to be our fate!

"I don't care," I said, and Jasper nodded in agreement. *"I'll do whatever it takes."*

Discover the entire award-winning "Grim Hill" Series

The Secret of Grim Hill

978-1-897073-53-7

Uncover the secret that started it all! This suspenseful tale pits Cat Peters and her friends against diabolical fairies and their powerful spells in a Halloween showdown.

Grim Hill, Book 2
The Secret Deepens

978-1-897073-97-1

Sookie's dabbling in magic unleashes a brutal winter and a strange sickness, and forces Cat to return to the last place she wants to go – Grim Hill!

www.grimhill.com

Grim Hill, Book 3
The Forgotten Secret

978-1-897550-13-7

Valentine's Day is right around the corner, so it seems only natural that Cat's friends, her sister, and even her soccer coaches have all been captivated by romance. But even romance has a sinister side in a town with Grim Hill at its center.

Grim Hill, Book 4
The Family Secret

978-1-897550-65-6

When Cat and her friends take part in a student exchange to Sweden, Cat uncovers an old family secret about fairy fighters and an ancient battle with Scandinavian fairy folk.

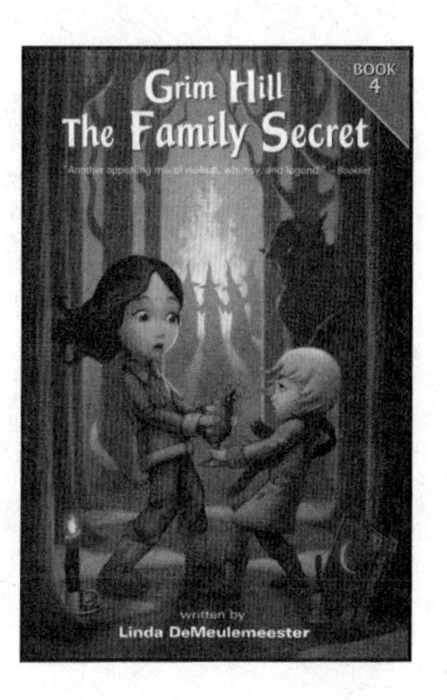

www.grimhill.com

About the Author:

Linda DeMeulemeester has worked in the fields of literacy and education for many years as a teacher and program adviser. She credits her grandmother, a natural storyteller who was born over a hundred years ago, for her love of mystery and suspense. Linda is a graduate of the Clarion West Workshop for writers of science fiction and fantasy, and her short stories have been published in several magazines. ***The Secret of Grim Hill*** was her first novel. Fans can connect with Linda at www.grimhill.com.